THE DAYDREAMER'S
DIARY

THE DAYDREAMER'S
DIARY

James Daunheimer

iUniverse LLC
Bloomington

THE DAYDREAMER'S DIARY

iUniverse books may be ordered through booksellers or by contacting:

iUniverse LLC
1663 Liberty Drive
Bloomington, IN 47403
www.iuniverse.com
1-800-Authors (1-800-288-4677)

ISBN: 978-1-4917-3009-6 (sc)
ISBN: 978-1-4917-3010-2 (e)

Library of Congress Control Number: 2014905638

Printed in the United States of America.

iUniverse rev. date: 03/27/2014

Acknowledgement Page:

The Grenier Sisters

CHAPTER ONE

Dreams. That's all Aiden Ellis could think about as he rushed past students. His heart rate increased with a little bit of moisture dripping upon his forehead as he swerved through the crowded hallways knowing his time was short. A loud bell jingled as Aiden stumbled past an unknown teacher's annoying eyes that looked freaky being as dark in the middle as any he's ever seen before.

A messy classroom was filled with noisy students who chatted away and threw crumbled papers at each other. The new substitute teacher then introduced himself with a subtle voice that kept the students blaring. He browsed around the room and took in all the faces before he looked at his roster filled with student's names. The teacher lowered his head viewing his thick sweater underneath his sport coat. He then lowered his head and noticed a small rip on the sweater just below his large collared shirt. He grabbed his corduroy coat and yanked it over a few inches. Students became quieter and started to stare at this strange looking teacher who was wearing layers of clothing similar to winter wear.

The teacher looked around the room and held his eyebrows low. "Open your Civics' books to page eighty-nine; we need to review this chapter before the test tomorrow!"

"Ah!" The class let out before they opened their books and slumped within their chairs. The teacher then chose a student in the back of the room to begin reading from the start of the chapter. The student's face immediately drooped before he opened his textbook and flung through the pages followed by his dull voice that read off the words.

A few minutes into the chapter recital Aiden remembered and understood all the content. He sat in the library two days ago and read the entire chapter but never thought he'd remember one bit of it. This astonished him to a smile.

History was an enjoyable subject that Aiden actually enjoyed. He then sprung-up a memory of seeing Meghan that day in the library. Yes, Meghan. The only girl who sent shivers down his spine with feelings he never felt before. She sat two tables away in class and passed several notes to the girls. There was something about Meghan, her looks, her character, stature, and movements . . . he just couldn't grasp.

Still hearing the textbook being recited, Aiden turned his head and glimpsed around the classroom. Several of the boys in the back row scribbled on their notebooks as they slithered deep into their chairs. The majority of girls sat in the middle of the class, many passed notes to each other by throwing down a folded paper to the floor and kicking it over. All was the same.

Aiden just didn't have any close friends in school; it was only the teens that needed something with no return. To the front of the class sat the geeky ones who just loved being in school and got many A's on their report cards. Aiden's interests were there, he just couldn't find his forte with those ones.

Aiden then internally giggled as the teacher sat back in his chair and stared at his textbook. His facial expressions glared like a droll as if he wasn't familiar with this history book. The full-time teacher always stared at the class and scrunched her eyes at the students who didn't pay attention.

Aiden started to yawn as he glanced down to his desk. Last night just seemed to drag with numerous times awake. He placed his left arm on to the windowsill and stared outside viewing these beautiful blue skies. A few bubble shaped clouds floated high and moved slowly. There were multi-leveled open fields behind the school that were mostly brown while others looked a little greener.

A brisk breeze moved the soccer goal netting and stirred Aiden's view over to the spouting buds along the tree line. Within that tree line, he could see a couple of dogs congregating near a mildewed old rock wall. He then recognized that one was a German Sheppard.

Aiden looked back up into the sky and noticed the clouds moving a bit faster and forming many shapes. A thin cloud to the left twisted in many directions, not to mention looked funny, because he remembered seeing jets creating similar clouds through their exhaust.

Directly outside the window he noticed leaves and other items that blew amongst the grass. Then a sudden notice of movement peaked interest. A steady and slower pace narrowed Aiden's vision. It was a turtle. Its shell had some bright yellow colored spots that were smooth and shined of light. He just couldn't make out what those spots looked like.

Aiden rested his chin upon his hand as the turtle walked peacefully amongst the grass. *Wait a minute, why is that turtle there and not anywhere near a lake or stream?* This question quickly took over Aiden's thoughts with no answer. He knew there was a stream down the hill, but that was quite a walk for anyone, not to mention days for this turtle.

Was there an owner near by, maybe a professor or teacher? Aiden looked in both directions hoping to see a person near the turtle—no one in sight.

As Aiden looked farther back he saw dogs start to dash across the distant field. They both stayed close together and had their tongues whipping all over the place. Suddenly, the dogs turned to the right and looked as though they were headed straight for the building. This intrigued Aiden as they got closer, but he then realized who they might run into or encounter. The turtle!

Aiden felt his heart rate increase as he looked up and down several times. The turtle still headed to the left and probably towards that far stream while the dogs passed in front of each other and got closer to the turtle.

Oh, this isn't happening. Aiden thought.

This turtle is not as fast as those squirrels but it sure does have a shell. Aiden just couldn't figure out why all the turtles he saw were alone without friends or family? Maybe that shell is another reason or excuse why that turtle is alone. Aiden let out a big sigh and began to feel at ease as he stared out the glossy window . . .

"Aiden . . . Aiden Ellis!" The teacher shouted louder as he stared straight at him.

Gathering his reality by seeing brown and green grass fields, Aiden realized he was daydreaming. He then instantly thought of that turtle and raised himself higher within his chair and just couldn't see that little one anywhere on the grass.

"Are you feeling ok Aiden?" Mr. Tormey said with a questionable glare.

The whole class chuckled as he sat back down and moved his head around the class noticing everyone's faces just staring and laughing at him. Aiden looked back to the front where he saw the teacher pointing his finger down into the textbook and smirking aggressively at him.

"Please start reading the next paragraph." Teacher said.

Aiden recognized the two open pages. He knew what they all said, but wasn't sure which paragraph he was supposed to read. Beginning to feel a little nervous, while continuously looking at both pages, he just started reading out loud a paragraph on the bottom.

The class roared louder. Aiden stopped reading and raised his eyes to notice Mr. Tormey leaning back in his chair with his arms resting behind his head. The school bell then started to ring and the whole class grabbed their books and scuttled towards the door.

"Alright class, everyone read that chapter again tonight. Got a test tomorrow!" Teacher said watching the kids' head out the door. He then looked directly at Aiden who was placing his book inside his bag and beginning to head towards the door. "I need to talk with you for few minutes."

Coming to a halt and still staring at the door Aiden lowered his head and headed towards the front desk. With this head still facing down he raised his eyes a couple of times. Mr. Tormey never moved his eyes.

"Please take a seat."

A chair was pulled closer to the desk.

"Are you alright?"

Aiden raised his head and looked right into Mr. Tormey's eyes. This was the normal question that every teacher asked. It was shocking that a teacher asked this question on his first day. This intrigued Aiden and also made him wonder about himself before he let that thought dissolve within a second or two.

"I'm fine."

"You are either not feeling well or just not all there today?"

"I'm feeling fine."

"Well then, I guess you are not all there today. Look Aiden, you must have been thinking about something because when I asked you to read a paragraph you interpreted one that was already read several pages before. I'm only asking you this because I can help you if you need it."

"I promise I'm fine." Aiden said with an unemotional face.

Mr. Tormey leisurely winked. "Ok, I have one question for you. What state was Thomas Jefferson raised in?"

"Virginia." Aiden responded quickly while standing up.

Mr. Tormey raised his eyelids and looked surprised about how fast that answer came. Aiden got close to the door before he stopped and turned around.

"Thomas Jefferson was buried in Monticello, Virginia in 1826."

Aiden then turned again and walked out the door. Mr. Tormey sat there in amazement and shook his head while smiling before seeing the new class enter through the door.

As he walked down the crowded hallway Aiden suddenly felt strange with his heart bumping faster and his forehead becoming warmer. For many moments he's been adrift from remembering so many events that he finally realized report cards were mailed already. Then thoughts of what might happen tonight when his mother opened that report card left him with a sense of dread. Why did this have to ruin my day?

Aiden knew his next class was a study break. He then knew he only had a few seconds to make it to the library across the courtyard leading to the other side of the school. Once that class finished, he then knew he was heading home and had to plan a way of getting that report card before his mother saw it.

CHAPTER TWO

In front of his house, Aiden opened the mailbox and noticed it empty. He then leaned back and noticed a red Chevy convertible parked in the side lot. Nana was visiting and this meant a challenge to capture his report card. He opened the porch door, walked to the end, and stared out of the window not seeing another car in the lot. He was nervous knowing Nana looked after his activities for mom.

"Welcome home Aiden." Nana said as he closed the inside door.

Aiden dropped his bag behind the chair and threw his coat along its arm.

"So how was school today?" She kept her eyes down while knitting a new quilt.

"It was OK."

They sat in silence for a few minutes until the doorbell rang.

"Oh my goodness that was startling." Nana looked over and tapped her feet as Aiden stared down to the floor. "Are you going to get the door?"

"Yes." Aiden scraggily rose to his feet and opened the door.

He walked out on to the porch and opened the door where a mailman handed him a large envelope. Aiden knew this was an opportunity but also knew he wasn't going to get away with it. When the door finally closed Aiden placed the envelope upon the coffee table. He sat back down on the chair and slumped further down.

"So, what is that Aiden?"

"It's for Mom." He glanced over at Nana.

Nana squinted her eyes tighter but just couldn't read the words upon the envelope. She then looked at Aiden with an interesting stare.

"Are you OK?"

"Yes."

"You sure are quiet and look like something is wrong."

"I wish it was Friday."

"Friday's are fun knowing two restful days are ahead."

Aiden then formed an inquisitive stare towards Nana, quilting needles were moving so fast, and it was amazing how good she was. He has two quilts on his bed and three in his closet. He then realized Nana was in the house on Thursday, she usually came on Fridays.

"Is everything OK Nana?"

"Thanks for asking Aiden. I am fine." She looked at him quickly with a smile and then reached forward into the canvass quilt bag to grab more yarn.

Aiden looked around at the clock and noticed it was quarter after four. He reminded himself that he normally cooked dinner and that he would have to make more since Nana was here.

"Are you staying tonight?"

"Yes. I'm staying here this weekend as well."

Aiden then wondered why Nana was in the house a day early. It's been several days since her last stay and she normally arrived on Friday. This seemed obvious to Aiden that Nana was asked something from mom.

"Have you talked with Mom today?"

"She called me this morning and asked if I could watch you tonight."

"Why tonight?"

"Her boss asked if she could back-up some things tonight. She mentioned that she wouldn't be home till at least eight o'clock."

Aiden let out a large breath. His lips vibrated loudly. Nana raised her eyebrow.

"Your mother is a busy woman. She has a lot to handle being a single mother."

"I know Nana. She's an Information Systems Operations Programmer."

Nana shot an impressive glance, while still knitting.

"You are her world and Katie just has a lot on her plate."

"I know her job is hard. She rewrites the Finance and Costing Systems with inputs by keypunched cartridge cards. The cartridge holds many floppy's and must be backed-up."

"You are impressive Aiden. Sounds like you're speaking a foreign language."

"When I miss Mom I walk down the street to Texon."

"You sure read many of her technical books. Maybe they should hire you." Nana smiled.

"That stuff seems boring too me."

"It may be boring but it sure fills the refrigerator."

"I get your point." Aiden's eyes drooped lower as he frowned.

He walked into the kitchen and noticed the mail on the counter. He was forbidden to touch the mail—got in trouble many times for opening it. He then opened the refrigerator and scanned the rows where he saw many items. He then wandered through the cabinets for a while, keeping the refrigerator contents in mind.

"What are you in the mood for dinner tonight Nana?"

"Anything you feel like eating. Just make sure you are safe with the stove."

Aiden frowned again. Nana said that all the time. He remembered the first time he cooked for his Mother, she told the whole family and Nana has expected him cooking ever since. A few months ago, Aiden asked for Nana's help, she helped pick the ingredients but then sat and watched him cook. He just couldn't understand that.

Back in the refrigerator, he pulled out a large onion, a package of mushrooms, sour cream, and the beef round that he took out of the freezer last night. Putting the pan on stove, while hearing the gas click to flame, Aiden tossed the beef in. Knowing the tears would start flowing, he turned his head to the side while cutting the onions.

He then looked at the mail again and wondered if the report card was there. Throwing the onions in the pan, he clapped his hands, and then wiped a towel. Grabbing a spatula, Aiden then stepped closer to the mail. He wanted to forget about the mail, and return to his cooking. He tried again to concentrate on the beef, and it's browning, but there was something in his worries that wouldn't allow him to do so.

He stepped closer, and made his way through the mail. Once again, he perceived the many troubles about messing with this, he was told numerous times to leave it alone. This time his mother was at work and it was the mail that became important.

"What are you doing?" Nana said aggressively.

"Nothing." Aiden froze.

"You know better than to look through the mail. I still remember how angry Katie became when you threw out her bills. It hurt her and she still mentions that."

"I'm expecting a letter," Aiden gently said. "I was told that today."

"Who told you that?"

"A friend of mine."

"Just wait till your mother gets home and passes that."

"OK."

Aiden's face turned red as he walked back and flipped the beef over.

"That smells wonderful. What are you making for dinner?"

"Beef Stroganoff."

"I'm impressed." Nana said, as she walked in and put her hand upon Aiden's back.

He then shivered feeling her hand.

"Are you OK Aiden?"

"Yes."

Aiden walked over pulled a measurement cup off the counter and filled it with water. He knew Nana wouldn't stop asking if he showed aggression. He then thought of her quilt.

"Who are you making the quilt for Nana?"

"Oh, that quilt is for Sister Mary Gervais at Mont Marie Health Care Center. That's the Nun you talk with when you go to work with me."

"That's great. You know her favorite color is orange. I only see brown and green yarn on the quilt."

"Wonderful Aiden. I'm so glad you said something about her color. I never knew that."

"Yeah, she showed me many pictures one day and told me that."

"By the way, Katie asked if you could go to work with me the following weekend at Mont Marie."

"Why that weekend?"

"I work two weekends a month cleaning Mont Marie, but you know that and have been there before with me."

"I thought you meant this weekend."

"Oh." Nana said, seeing Aiden's face look discouraging.

"Dad called and told Mom that he will see me the second weekend in May."

"When did he tell your Mother that?"

"My birthday. He also told me on the phone that day."

"I hope it's the Saturday, because this weekend's Sunday is Mother's Day and you need to be with your Mother. Have you heard from him since then?"

Aiden felt flustered and scared. "No. Why? Was dad supposed to call again? Is something happening?"

"Calm down, I was only asking."

"Why?"

"It's OK. All I'm saying is that you can go to work with me the following weekend. I just hope your father makes it here this Saturday."

"He won't be busy, he said he'll be here!"

"Please calm down Aiden and relax. Do you need any help with dinner?"

Aiden then twitched. He never heard Nana ask him about help for dinner. He knew something was wrong.

"No thanks. I'm sure that quilt for Sister Gervais needs more time?"

"You are right, that quilt will take more time seeing how I have to add orange yarn into it."

Chapter Three

"Hello mom," said Katie entering the front door and putting her purse down on the couch. "I finally got that work done."

"Hi there Katie," said Nana looking at the clock. "You are ten minutes early."

"I'm shocked that I got that work done early, even tonight."

"Does that mean you have tomorrow off?"

"Yeah right. When was the last time I had one of those?" Said Katie moving her head along the back of the couch.

"True."

Katie leaned forward and saw Aiden sitting at the end of the dinning room table. The books were scattered along the table but his eyes looked glazy as he stared out the window. She thought that, with some patience, he'd be studying hard.

"Hello Aiden!"

With the startled wink, Aiden displayed a curious look then smiled.

"You know Katie, your son made a delicious dinner." Nana smiled.

"Did he?"

"He made one of my favorites, beef stroganoff. He sure has talent."

"He does."

Walking into the room Katie saw that Aiden looked tired. It was eight o'clock.

"I have a plate for you in the refrigerator." Aiden said before he yawned.

"Thanks honey." Katie kissed his forehead. "Please go get your pajamas on and brush your teeth."

"Ok."

Aiden gathered the books, packed them away, and headed to his bedroom. Katie then saw the stack of mail and thought more bills were in that pile. She grabbed and sat on a dinning chair, tossing the junk mail, until she noticed the Middle School return address. Her facial expression quickly changed after she opened and read the report card.

In his pajamas, Aiden headed toward the bathroom and noticed his mother reading mail. He was surprised then irritated. He didn't need to be in the house at this time. He closed the door and brushed his teeth. Then he slowed down knowing abruptness would be confronted leaving the bathroom. He then opened the door and walked fast.

"Aiden!"

He stopped while still facing his bedroom and felt his mother's eyes staring at him.

"Please come over and have a seat."

Aiden slowly pulled the chair and sat at the table.

"This is your report card." Mom tossed it across the table.

Aiden grabbed and started to read the report card. The first grade stated a 'B', the next 'D', then 'F', along with other failures. As he read back to the top he noticed History was the good one. He just didn't want to stop looking at the card knowing what mother was going to say.

Meanwhile, his mother leafed through several other pages without seeming to want the report card back. Aiden noticed his mother's emotions looked calm and not angry. She just looked tired; the bags under her eyes were swollen.

She was disappointed. Aiden decided that he would never again let his attention get distracted in school. He remembered that he had a number of things she discussed already—ones he just didn't stick with. Mom stared straight into his eyes.

"What is wrong?"

"I don't know what you mean."

"Of course you do." Mom frowned. "We talked about your last report card, one with better grades than this. It just seems your thoughts are all over the place. Maybe something else is happening to you that I have no clue about. Then again, it could be my fault since I'm hardly here with you."

Mom was saying strange things—Aiden thought. Sometimes it's better to be daydreaming because those dreams don't say anything when I'm by myself. Those daydreams tell their incredible stories at the time you want to remember them. When you're not enjoying them they have some influences that are so strange that you don't know how to continue.

"It's not you Mom." Aiden said softly, continuing to stare at report card.

"Then what is it honey?"

"I don't know."

"I have this long letter." Said Mom, holding it up. "The school counselor states that several teachers claim you pay little attention to them, you just stare out the window and think of other things."

"That's not true Mom!"

"Of course it is Aiden, these grades prove that."

"I always pay attention in History."

"That's not the only course you take." Mom let out a breath. "There are many courses we all take in school. It's called learning."

"I know that Mom."

"Just relax and tell me what is distracting you at school? Is it a bully, a girl, maybe some other issues?"

Mom stopped and closed her eyes. She looked so tired and normally couldn't get the work out of her head for several hours. Taking a deep breath Mom looked like she cleared her thoughts and opened her eyes.

"When I see you stare out of windows, or not listen to what I'm saying, I know you're thinking of something. Please tell me what is happening during those times?"

Aiden wondered for a few minutes and kept his mother's eyes in sight. He listened to the TV in the other room and felt like he was watching it. He tried to deal with the concept of daydreams as distinct from real life and couldn't separate them. But Mom was a person who listened. If anything could help him to understand it was a dream.

As Aiden sat thinking he sensed movement in front of him. Looking up, he saw Nana quietly walking past and towards the bathroom.

He watched and followed her strange movement like she wanted to be hidden. Maybe the way she was moving, and attempting to be hidden, could explain his solitude.

A sudden confusion alert then sounded within him. In his mind he wanted to know the problem, but he also enjoyed it as well. Knowing his mother needed an answer scared him, he just felt daydreams were right.

"I'm daydreaming. I don't know why, it just happens."

"OK, that's an answer and one that makes sense?" Mom's expression got livelier. "What are you daydreaming about?"

"Several things."

"Do you remember most of them?"

"Of course."

"Are they all the same or different?"

"Well." Aiden hesitated for a few seconds. "Both. I guess it depends."

"On what?"

"I don't know Mom."

"Can you tell me about them?"

"When?"

"All night long." Mom started to chuckle. "How about this weekend?"

"What happens if I can't remember them all?"

"Do you remember most?"

"I guess."

Katie then wondered if this was the best way to handle this situation. She knew Aiden would talk; it's not that he's lying or guessing at the correct story. The daydreams belong to Aiden, and it's only he who can reveal it, under his circumstances. How does guessing handle this? The secret is in his thoughts. If you pay attention to the daydreams you can correctly present them. If he can improve on revealing what he dreams later it may be better. It needs to never be forgotten!

"OK. Here's the punishment for your poor grades and lack of attention in class . . ." Katie halted, stood, and opened a cabinet drawer. Placing a hard cover notebook in front of Aiden she then sat down. "This notebook is now yours. You will take it wherever you go. That means it never leaves you. Now, most importantly, I want you to write down everything you remembered in your daydreams and all future ones you have. By no means are you to skip any, they will all be written. Does that make sense?"

"I guess." Said Aiden staring at the bright red notebook. Katie then yawned.

"Go get some sleep kiddo. It's getting late and we both have full days tomorrow."

Aiden nodded his head as he stumbled toward the bedroom.

CHAPTER FOUR

Computer processors buzzed as Katie opened her office glass door. She placed her purse under the desk, sat back in her chair, and yawned. Thoughts of Aiden kept her stirring most of the night.

Her decision forcing Aiden to write down his daydreams concerned her. She knew it was best, just hoped it didn't overtake his daily thoughts. Aiden is the jewel in her life and she contemplated any decision she had to make in reference to her son. She grudgingly punished him before but this concerned her greatly due to it possibly continuing his bad grades. However, it could bring back his focus to pay attention in classes. The unknown future months unsettled Katie.

Katie folded her hands under her chin. She viewed around the office seeing the floppy drives spin in circles. Gently opening her hands, as she settled her fingers on the keyboard, Katie tapped a few times and saw her monitor lighten. Today's input was larger than normal with a stack of keypunched cards. The IBM System/34 hard drive was under maintenance yesterday and Katie knew she had additional data to input into her terminal.

She noticed a note on her desk, one with flowered prints along the sides. These notes were Julie's, her co-worker. Katie let out a deep breath—most of Julie's notes meant sick day or appointments. She hesitated reading that note and didn't want all this additional work in her lap.

She grabbed her coffee cup and headed out the door. Warm caffeine was needed for energy. As she walked through the brightly lit and quiet hallway, Katie turned into the large break room. She then winked with remorse. The coffee pot was off with a tiny leftover amount. She pulled the pot and dumped it into the sink. As she filled the pot with water Katie realized she was the first one at work. She then remembered nicely asking everyone to empty and clean the coffee pot but knew they didn't listen. The looks on their faces made her feel it was expected of her.

Katie felt she worked for a company that was male dominated. She heard from friends, who worked in finance, that most men salaried more than her for equivalent work. She knew she wasn't a woman's liberator just the company's feminist. When woman around the company saw Katie stand for herself and bring her problems to the company president they spoke highly to her. The company CEO was friendly and always open-mindedly listened to Katie. Those conversations made her frustrations reduce. She just never saw those problems get resolved.

As she measured the coffee grounds Katie heard footsteps get closer. She tapped the measuring cup and poured it into the filter. The footsteps stopped in the doorway.

"Good morning Katie. That coffee is sure needed this morning."

Katie kept her head still. "Good morning Michael."

She pressed the 'ON' button, grabbed a towel, and wiped the counter clean. She knew Michael was still standing in the doorway; his Old Spice cologne lingered throughout the room. Katie smiled back. Michael Motyka's dark blonde hair was combed back and feathered over his ears then stared into his light blue eyes. That look combination attracted her, she just never showed it too him. Michael worked down the hallway, in the contracting department, and walked around the office several times a day to stretch his legs. He limped on occasion and only when his war wound from Vietnam acted up. Michael gracefully raised his hand and pointed low.

"Your shoes are pretty. They sure do look comfortable."

Katie looked down. "Thanks. I got them this past weekend after deciding to trash all those worn out shoes I've worn for many years."

"Hope they didn't cost too much?" Michael raised an eyebrow.

Katie's cheeks blushed. "They were affordable. Big sale this weekend."

"How's Aiden doing?"

Katie then grew a serious expression. She turned her head hearing the coffee maker gurgle.

"Is everything alright Katie?" Michael stepped forward.

"Yes. Aiden's fine." She swung her head slowly and took a breath. "I don't want to get down into the weeds with this one . . ." She hesitated. "It's just that Aiden's thoughts have been all over the place. His grades are dropping and his attitude lately just doesn't seem normal. Guess I'm just worried and don't know how to handle it."

Michael clinched his lips. "Aiden's only what?" He tilted his head. "Eleven years old? That's puberty sprouting physical and emotional pieces."

"He just turned twelve a few weeks back. But he's still Aiden in every wonderful way. It's just . . ." Katie hesitated. "It's just kind of disturbing how much he's been dreaming during the day. He doesn't concentrate enough in his classes hence the poor grades."

"That does sound interesting Katie. To be honest, I was a sleeper around that age. My teenager years were spent asleep on the bed." Michael smiled. "My parents would rip the sheets off and roll me out of bed to wake me up."

Katie heard the coffee pot beep. She reached for the pot. "You want some coffee?"

"Please."

Michael held his cup out with a stiff arm. Katie felt the heavy pot and wanted to make sure she didn't spill. She grabbed it tighter and then put her hand softly over Michael's hand. She held his cup steady as she poured. Michael grinned.

"Thanks."

Katie poured into her cup. "How's your daughter Meghan doing?"

"Meghan is doing well . . . in grades that is. She just seems to be attached to our home phone talking about nothing all night long."

"Does that bother you?"

"A little. But to be honest with you it sure keeps her safe in the house."

Katie smiled while she dripped cream into her cup. "I can understand what you're saying. If I remember correctly Meghan just turned thirteen?"

"She sure did. March twenty-first. I will have to dust off the shackles and shotgun for her future dates." Michael sarcastically squinted his eyes while smirking.

Katie shook her head with a grin. She then heard another set of footsteps that walked down the hallway. Michael bent backwards and looked over.

"Good morning Mr. Sordun."

"Hello Michael. That coffee smell dragged me this way."

Katie saw Michael back into the hallway as Mr. Sordun entered the room. His suave appearance and behavior always looked professional. Something bright reflected from his chest, drawing Katie's eyes. Mr. Sordun always wore an American flag tie clip.

"Good morning Katie."

Katie smiled. "Good morning."

She pulled the coffee pot and poured Mr. Sordun's cup. He grinned and always looked as though his brain was spinning with laboring thoughts. Katie liked his personality she just never trusted his corporate persona.

"Thanks Katie. How are things in the information systems office?"

Katie shot Mr. Sordun a glare as she placed the coffee pot on the counter. "You really want to know?"

Mr. Sordun smirked knowing Katie was honest. "Of course I do."

"We are behind in imputing the increased data into finance and costing systems. That amount has increased significantly and Julie and I are working overtime hours. Two programmers aren't enough." Katie smiled with closed lips and speedy blinks.

"I understand Katie. We recently signed another contract adding increased product development. Your shop isn't the only one undermanned." Mr. Sordun sipped his coffee. "How are things with you Katie?"

"With overtime hours and my additional security duty I really haven't been happy coming to work."

"Security duty." Who put you on that duty?"

"The facility manager did. I live five houses down the street and often get called late at night for alarms and security personnel who locked their keys in the buildings.

In addition, I'm also in charge of file retention for on and off premises."

Mr. Sordun took another sip of coffee. "No problem Katie. I will place those duties on the appropriate people." He then back stepped through the door. "Please have a good day and know that your inputs will be reviewed by me."

Katie watched him dart quickly down the hallway. She then saw Michael bend his head through the door and smile. Another woman slowly passed by the door and glared at Katie. That woman was a true gossiper.

Walking back to her office, Katie noticed two ladies quietly chatting in the hallway. When they saw Katie, both women hushed. Katie didn't care. She hated gossip. She opened the office door and heard the ladies laugh.

The rest of the day was eventful as Katie expected. Her desk was piled with keypunched cards. She only worked half the stack. Katie knew she could've imputed faster but believed it best to do it correctly and avoid corrections. She looked at her watch and rubbed her teeth together. It was six thirty at night. The last time she looked it was three o'clock and that seemed like a few minutes ago.

CHAPTER FIVE

Katie felt her blood pressure rise. She knew it was Friday and Aiden usually got home around four o'clock. She quickly ran around the office, backed computer disks and stored them. She then locked her system and grabbed her purse. The door locked smoothly. She double tapped the lock, it didn't move. She walked through the offices and noticed the lights off and parking lot empty. When she reached the foyer—the building main entrance—she punched the security code and walked out. The beep-beep sounded loudly and she heard the outer door click.

As she walked down the sidewalk Katie observed the house. The house had three apartments, two on top floor and one on bottom floor. Her father was good friends with the owner and referred Katie to rent from him. The family helped her and Aiden move into the bottom floor apartment, one that her furniture was comfortable in.

She was then stunned. The two Doberman Pincher's across the street, in the fenced driveway, barked up a storm. Katie endured their piercing barks every day on her way home. She normally prepared herself to deal with the barks but her focus was now Aiden.

She noticed the window blinds were raised. Katie knew Aiden was home. This comforted her but still wished she called him earlier. She normally called around five o'clock daily to make sure all was well or to see what Aiden was cooking for dinner. When she was busy Katie either got a phone call or saw Aiden walk into her office. This created many uncertain thoughts of not seeing or hearing from him today. Those thoughts petrified Katie.

As she opened the front door Katie noticed the television was off in the living room. She walked into the dining room and glanced into the kitchen where she saw the light under the door where Nana was staying. She knocked lightly and heard a "Hello" from her mother. Katie then walked back into the dinning room and looked around. She felt alarmed not seeing Aiden. Her blood pressure rose.

"Aiden!" Katie shouted as she headed for the bedrooms.

"Hi mom. I'm in my bedroom."

Katie slowed down and smiled. She poked her head into his bedroom and saw him sitting on his bed writing into the notebook. He looked comfortable and shook his feet while quietly whistling to himself.

"What time did you get home?"

"A few minutes ago." Aiden said as he kept writing.

Katie clenched her teeth. "Honey, it's quarter to seven."

"What do you mean?" Aiden looked over at his clock and raised his eyebrows. "I was here after four o'clock when I started writing."

Katie smiled. "Time sure does pass when you're busy. I can second that."

"I guess."

"Well, kiddo, I'm sorry I'm late. Today was just too much for me." Katie took a deep breath while her stomach growled. "Have you eaten anything for dinner?"

Aiden shook his head left to right and continued to write. Katie felt strange. She normally would lecture or ostracize Aiden for not correctly answering her. However, he looked enthralled writing his punished assignment. There was just an uncertain facial expression that backed her initial thought and one she hoped would make things better.

Katie went into her bedroom, changed into comfy wear, and threw her clothes into the full hamper. She grabbed the handle and dragged down the hallway to the washer. Without a stranger being in the house Katie felt it best to release her anger with laundry—her best solution.

She opened the washer and aggressively tossed pieces in. With only a few left in the hamper, frustration still inside, she swore tossing in the last. The washer drawer was slammed as Katie hit a few buttons and heard the water flow. She leaned down on her elbows, wrapped her hands upon her face, and took a few breaths. She then felt her thoughts get cheerful. She didn't know why, just felt well, and that's all that mattered to her. Katie giggled as she closed the hamper. There were days when this stress relief didn't work but that wasn't today because she felt calm and stood tall.

Katie knew she needed to eat something her stomach ached with hunger. She walked into the kitchen and opened the cabinets and refrigerator. After she knocked on the door and asked Nana, she was told her sister took her out for dinner. Katie leaned against the counter and wondered what dinner she was in for. Her normal dinner items just didn't seem flavorsome. She wanted something new or hasn't had in a while. As she contemplated her taste buds a sweet and sour taste arose. The closest Chinese restaurant was and another town away. All the meat was frozen and still in the freezer. It then dawned on her—she could mix pasta with vegetables. Why not?

As she diced the vegetables Katie boiled the pasta while frying the rest. She then drained the pasta and threw in the onions, peas, and mushrooms. As she mixed them together she poured the sweet and sour sauce into the pot and continued. It was fast and a taste Katie yearned for.

"Aiden, dinner is ready!"

Katie looked down the hallway and heard movement in his room. After she put the plates, silverware, and napkins on the table, Katie brought over the pot and rested it on top of a folded kitchen towel. Aiden strolled into the dining area, sat at the table, and placed his notebook down. Katie stared at the notebook and wondered what he wrote. Aiden lifted his plate and scooped the food out of the pot. He then put an appealing look upon his face.

"What's this?"

"It's a sweet and sour dinner."

Aiden slowly swerved his fork through the food as he stared down. Katie took a bite, leaned back, and shook her head. She noticed him still staring at his food.

"Take a bite, it's tasty."

Aiden looked up. He twirled his fork and took a bite. As he chewed slowly his face cleared of doubt. He chewed faster and opened his notebook. Katie saw him write a few sentences as she took another bite. The ecstatic look on his face increased Katie's feelings. Being home with her son was enough. Aiden being content and safe meant the world to her.

Katie took the time to observe moments within life and nature. It was in her blood. She reminisced back to her hard-working father who once sat her down to explain their surroundings. The lush greenery in summer and bare coldness in winter, her father explained the seasons and what that meant to their lives. She was his youngest daughter and one he privileged. Never were the moments long enough for Katie, she remembered all those short times like they were yesterday and respected her father for that.

Aiden's father, Stewart, was different. Whether he was too young, or overly focused in his rock band, he never was around to support his family. Katie knew her ex-husband's lack of observations and time. She just loved him. Soon after becoming pregnant they both eloped and moved in together.

Her love for him then quickly dwindled due to an empty marriage. Stewart constantly traveled on the road with his band. Katie's sisters gratefully supported her through pregnancy stages and depression. Her father never respected Stewart, he told Katie many times, even before she married, that her boyfriend didn't comprehend moments.

Katie's heart broke for Stewart when she gave birth. Aiden's precious face glowed deep into her heart. Her son was now the priority and one she cherished enough to observe forever. Her husband's life and focus never changed.

A few months after Aiden's birth Katie locked Stewart in the house. She explained what marriage was about and especially with a child. Stewart sat there motionless for hours. Katie took every verbal path she knew with no response. She finally put her foot down and cast an absolute question: "Does your son or your life take priority?" Katie gave him one day to respond. The next morning Stewart was gone and never left a note. That was that.

Katie looked over and noticed Aiden still writing in his notebook. She knew he was a focused boy and one who always completed projects he enjoyed. Unfortunately, he rarely completed projects he didn't enjoy. She then saw his plate empty, Katie internally giggled. Aiden normally didn't finish new dishes she made for him.

"Do you want anymore dinner?"

"No thank you." Aiden kept writing.

Katie took the plates into the kitchen. As she walked by the refrigerator the calendar on the door caught her attention. She set the plates into the sink and took a few steps backwards. Her fists then clenched as she bared her teeth. Tomorrow was Stewart's day with Aiden. Katie then felt some pressure in her forehead. Recently Stewart promised to stop by on Aiden's birthday and never showed. She called him numerous times and he never called back until the next day. Aiden answered that call and was excited that his father promised to take him to an amusement park in Agawam. Katie regretfully wrote that on the calendar too.

She flinched her head as Aiden coughed. Katie turned quickly and saw Aiden stretch his arms and go right back to writing in his notebook. With her blood pressure raised Katie considered calling Stewart. She knew it didn't matter though. Most phone call agreements were never held.

"I'm just going out to the parking lot for a cigarette." Katie said as she walked towards the back porch.

"OK."

Katie walked around in circles as she smoked her third cigarette. The sudden breeze was cool and fresh and her mind was elsewhere. Having to remind Aiden about tomorrow's conundrum bothered her greatly. She only wished Stewart showed but she highly doubted his arrival.

As she opened the door Katie noticed the house was dark. She wondered why Aiden didn't turn on any lights. The light under his bedroom door was bright but she didn't hear any radio or television. Katie raised her hand to knock on his door but halted. Her thoughts told her to remind him, she just felt it best not to knock.

Katie yawned. Her day was long and disturbing. Getting some sleep now took over her thoughts. To make sure the house was secure she walked to the front door and saw it locked. She then noticed Aiden's shoes on the floor. Hung over the chair laid his coat. Katie shook her head and felt her shoulders droop lower.

Aiden's waiting for tomorrow—Katie dreadfully thought. She remembered the last few times Stewart promised to see Aiden and didn't show. Stewart must own an excuse book.

Walking back to her bedroom Katie stared at Aiden's bedroom door. She passed by and thought him a good night sleep. Once Katie put on her pajamas, and peeled back her bed covers, she crossed her fingers and turned off the light.

Chapter Six

With a sunrise blooming through the window Aiden felt excited about spending the day with his father. He jumped out of bed and slowly opened his bedroom door. He knew his mother was still asleep and needed more. He lightly stepped to the bathroom and then heard a cough in the living room. Aiden swung his head over and saw the clock. It's six thirty in the morning and that meant Nana's been awake for at least an hour or two. He walked into the living room.

"Good morning Nana."

"Hello. How are you this morning?"

Aiden stood tall and felt his eyes get larger. "I'm great. My father will be picking me up soon and were going to Riverside Park."

Nana raised her eyebrow. "That amusement park is already open for the year?"

"Yes."

Nana took a sip of her coffee then went right back to reading her book. Aiden spun around and toddled into the kitchen. He felt hungry but knew his father would take him out for breakfast—that was mentioned several times in last phone call. As he opened the refrigerator Aiden grabbed the orange juice and filled a cup to the brim. He lightly stepped back in the bathroom and took a quick shower. He then frivolously combed the thick hair before stepping into his bedroom and tossing on clothes.

With his bedroom door slightly opened Aiden could hear a few snores coming from his Mother's room. He felt his lips form a masculine smile. She sure snored louder in the morning and Aiden was used to that, he knew it meant better sleep. There were plenty of nights he remembered being awake in the middle of the night and hearing her tip tap around the house. He wondered about Mom's lack of sleep many times but felt it best not to ask her.

As he headed toward the living room Aiden opened the closet and grabbed his winter coat because the coat he left in living room was too light. He knew this morning would be chilly and just a bit more than he could handle without a warmer coat. The temperature will climb greatly come noon time and Aiden knew he could toss in father's car before they head into the park.

Aiden stepped lightly when he entered the living room. He felt that Nana had some issue or problem when he first saw her this morning. Nana just didn't say much, she was that kind of woman who didn't criticize a situation unless it was severe or her opinion was asked.

Many months ago Aiden remembered jumping up-and-down loudly in his bedroom with a buddy of his. The music blasted at full volume. He never heard Nana enter the house but heard her scream loudly standing at his bedroom door. Aiden felt so petrified when he saw Nana's heated facial expression—one that a kid would remember and talk about for life. He loved Nana very much just never understood who she personally was with emotions.

Aiden saw the front door then looked over at Nana, she was deep within her book and sipping her coffee. He lightly stepped then decided to focus on the front door. As he turned the door handle Aiden heard a light cough.

"What time is your father picking you up?"

Aiden halted and spun his head. "He said eight o'clock this morning."

Nana raised her wrist and peeked at her watch. "It's only seven thirty." She lowered her book to her leg. "And it's still nippy outside. Why don't you wait inside until your father arrives I'm sure he will either honk or knock at the door." Nana pleasantly winked.

Aiden felt the blood rush through his veins. He was just too excited and felt his father would be arriving earlier. During the last phone call his father sounded firm and happy about the visit. Aiden just assumed that meant an early arrival.

"Father will be here soon Nana and taking me to breakfast."

Nana stared back into her book as she raised it higher.

"That's good news. I was just going to ask you if you ate something."

"I had some orange juice Nana."

"That's fine. Please knock at the door when he arrives or if you need anything."

Aiden gracefully beamed a smile. "I will Nana."

The door closed.

CHAPTER SEVEN

As Katie opened her eyes Nana was standing at the foot of the bed. "Are you positive that Stewart is coming today?" Nana's tone demanded an answer.

Katie sat up in bed and blinked her eyes several times. "Excuse me?"

"Stewart. That man just doesn't have reliability." She said, sounding very much like she was referring to a new breed of poisonous insects taking over the house.

Katie tried to poke herself awake. She lightly shook her head and began to feel somewhat conscious. Last night's sleep was hard and her head felt like a stone until the blood flowed faster.

"Where is Aiden?"

Nana fisted her hands to her hips. "He's sitting outside on the front steps."

Katie spun her head and noticed it was quarter till eight in the morning. She grabbed her sheets and threw them to the side of the bed. As she put her feet to the floor all Katie could feel is uncertainty. Any mention, or thought, of Stewart made her cringe and especially when that involved Aiden. She then quickly remembered having a hard time falling asleep last night due to knowing what today meant. Her son would possibly be shedding tears all day once his father never showed.

Katie was fine with Stewart never seeing Aiden again. There were many past incidents when Stewart never kept his word. Her divorce with Stewart, even before Aiden was a year old, proved that to her. Katie believed it was Stewart's world and everyone else just lived in it.

Katie then heard a constant beep down the hallway. Nana sat down beside her on the bed.

"The coffee is finished and I suggest you drink a cup before calling Stewart."

Katie raised and lowered her head silently. She knew that calling Stewart was the best way to know his location. The last few times Stewart promised to visit was halted when she called and he answered from his house in Upton, MA. That commute was about an hour drive. However, there were a few times when Katie did call with no answer and Stewart still didn't show.

Katie swallowed hard and stood to her feet before putting on her robe and heading toward the kitchen. Nana was right behind her, kept silent, and continued into living room.

As she entered the kitchen Katie starred at the phone for a few seconds. She then whirled herself around and grabbed a cup before filling it with coffee. After a few sips Katie stepped closer to the phone and tapped the counter a few times. She then lowered her cup.

Pushing the numbers on the phone felt like a dagger being poked into her fingers. She cringed every number but knew this was best for her son—the only reason she would sacrifice herself calling Stewart.

Katie remained silent as the phone rang several times. She closed her eyes for a moment. If Stewart answered she certainly had no plans to make this easy on him. She would present many unclean words to intently make herself feel better.

"Damn!" Katie said as she hung up the phone. The Stewart arrival situation was now a fifty percent chance or maybe worse since Katie experienced nothing but uncertainty in regards to Stewart.

Katie then raised her cup and sauntered angrily into the living room. So much anger and distrust, with such little power over stopping it, made Katie grieve this situation further. As she got closer to the front door Nana cleared her throat loudly.

"You think that's best Katie?"

Katie exhaled knowing that Nana spoke the truth. "I just want to strangle Stewart for not knowing his location."

"He's not here yet Katie." Nana put her book down and leaned forward. "Anything unknown or doubtful will make anybody angry. Hell, it's not anywhere near as important as this but just not knowing if my bowels will be regular everyday makes me angry."

Katie felt her eyebrows rise highly before Nana tapped the couch beside her.

"I know that mention was out there but hopefully you get my point?"

Katie sat down quickly with an inquisitive stare. "Are you having intestinal problems again?"

Nana blinked her eyes quickly. "OK, I shouldn't have used that as an example. I'm fine and pooping like a racer lately. Just fine thank you very much." Nana smirked. "What I'm trying to say is please relax and focus on Aiden not Stewart. Aiden is the only one we should be thinking about now."

Katie leaned back on the couch and sipped her coffee a few times. She looked across the living room and stared out the window while she contemplated what Nana mentioned. Only her mother knew how to handle Katie's emotions better than anyone. Aiden was a child who wanted to believe in his father. Katie made sure to always hold her words truthfully knowing the role of a parent was respect and truth.

Katie grinned at Nana. "You are right mother. I will just go out there and see how he's doing."

Nana leaned back and raised her book.

Katie raised herself diligently and opened the front door. She stepped upon the front porch and gazed out the window to see Aiden sitting upright amongst the front steps. He swiveled his head left and right glancing down the road. Katie then noticed the diary was upon his lap. She felt a rush of emotions dash through her system and for a moment Katie was sure that she was going to handle this day in a good manner.

As she opened the porch door Katie saw Aiden look back with a smile.

"Good morning mom."

"Good morning pumpkin. How are you holding up?" Katie said as she squatted next to him on the steps and instantly felt the coldness flow through her system. She tightened her robe around her waste as Aiden continued to glance down the road.

"I can't remember which way dad drives down this street."

"No worries. You father knows where the house is and will hopefully arrive soon." Katie muttered as she lightly placed her arm over his shoulder and sensed his exhilaration. "How about you come inside and watch some cartoons." She beamed at him as Aiden kept watching the road. "I believe Looney Tunes will be running now. You'll get to see Bugs Bunny and Daffy Duck."

Aiden blasted his eyes at mom for a second. "Taz is my favorite and they haven't shown him in two weeks."

Katie rubbed his shoulder and thought quickly before smiles abounded upon her.

"That Tasmanian Devil sure does spin and spit a lot. He's cute." Katie brought her hand down to Aiden's knee. "You may also see your favorite Schoolhouse Rock commercial. You know. "I'm just a Bill . . . sitting here at Capitol Hill. Mum . . . mum . . . mum! That cartoon character is cute with that red, white, and blue button that says 'Bill'."

Aiden closed his eyelids for a few seconds and smirked a tiny smile. "My new favorite is Hanker for a Hunk of Cheese."

Katie winced back and giggled. "I hanker for a hunka, a slab or slice or chunka, I hanker for a hunk of cheese."

Aiden pleasantly smiled, then chuckled loudly, staring back at Katie. She reached around him and hugged in closely. Those few seconds of hugs felt like hours of joy to Katie.

CHAPTER EIGHT

Aiden loved being hugged, especially by his mother. The muscles in the back of his neck loosened as she smiled at him. His mother took light breaths as she told funny stories and made him feel more secure. There were many emotional downsides that he remembered about his mother, and only his mother, reviving him back to normal. He never contemplated it much and he knew deep down inside that his mother was his best friend.

Meanwhile, Aiden closed his eyes and contemplated performing a silent prayer hoping his father would arrive, but as usual still no answer. It didn't matter though he still believed his father would show. The longer he sat on the steps the more his thoughts ambled into others.

A few neighbors walked by earlier and greeted him but also asked if everything was OK. Aiden properly waved and responded then felt guilty for not paying the appropriate attention as he kept staring down the road. He knew things were fine and wondered why he reacted that way. Too much thought and so many what ifs. His father engulfed his feelings. He just didn't know how to think about it without getting confused.

All of a sudden a roaring engine got louder as a car turned the corner. Aiden knew it wasn't his father's car, but it made him reflect upon, god brother, Donny's renovated late 1960s Chevrolet Chevelle—the one he loved riding in. The internal seat shook, equaling the 350 horse powered engine rumble, and that felt amazing. The power alone meant a grown person possibly adult. He didn't understand why this event made him feel that way. He didn't care. All he sought after were people he knew seeing him in the passenger seat. The astounded or annoyed looks were enough to make Aiden beam adult feelings. He felt like a man in that car.

Aiden sucked in a deep breath. The sun was rising fast as the warmth increased. He unzipped his coat and took another deep breath. His attention dwindled and thoughts swayed all over the place . . .

The parking lot was filled to the brim as casually dressed people walked faster to the Daytona 500 International Speedway entrance. The weather was perfect as Aiden held hands with his mother and heard recognizable chatter behind him. As he turned his head back he noticed his Auntie Susie and Bonnie along with his cousin's Danny and John. After he locked-up the rental car uncle Don lit up his cigar and casually caught up to the family pack.

Aiden squinted around for his father. A familiar numbness showered through him knowing his father probably wasn't there. It felt normal.

But then . . .

Excitement intensified hearing the loud engines roar. Either the car's crews, or drivers, were testing their engines or were spinning around the raceway. A thunderous crowd cheered, whistled, and stomped the seating area floors. Thump, thump, thump!

As they got closer to the entrance Aiden saw and smelt the wood smoke from the food trailer directly in front of him. After the family members passed through the ticket counter, Aiden stared at a sign above the food trailer. "Southern BBQ Burger" lettering was the biggest upon the sign. He felt his tummy rumble and so desired a cheeseburger. The greasy burger taste was definitely his priority.

Aiden pulled his mother's shirt and pointed to the sign. After she looked-up his mother smiled and intently blinked her eyes. He took her looks as an approval. He ran quickly to the counter and ordered the burger. A woman wearing a red and checkered jersey handed him a covered thick plastic plate. Aiden grinned and thanked the woman before he unwrapped the paper and saw darkly colored orange and red sauce exude over the buns. He lengthened the distance—what he thought was a burger—from his eyes and felt his mouth drop open and eyes widen. This burger was shredded meat.

Aiden lifted the shredded burger to his nose and inhaled a large hot and sweet smell. He was shocked and never seen or smelled such a burger. Confusion made him believe he was handed the wrong order. He stepped back to the counter.

"Excuse me miss. I ordered the Southern BBQ Burger and this doesn't look like a burger."

The woman blinked and jetted out a heavy southern accent. "It sure is cutie."

Aiden peeked down into his plastic plate, one that was getting moist. He jetted a confused look as the woman grinned.

"It's grounded and smoked hamburger meat cooked in our special BBQ sauce." The woman put her hands on her hips. "Where are you from cutie?"

"I'm visiting from Massachusetts."

The woman chuckled. "That sure explains it cutie. Go ahead and enjoy that tasty Southern BBQ Burger. It's best to try new tastes when you travel."

Aiden shrugged his shoulders. "Thanks." He then turned around and caught up with his family who got closer to the speedway's left side entrance.

A sudden bright light emblazoned his view and before he knew it he was sitting on a grandstand seat closest to turn four along the speedway. He blinked his eyes greatly before he saw the immense raceway, one that was massive compared to anything he ever saw at hometown raceway in Agawam, MA.

A loud announcement then echoed across the stands. The race was about to begin. People screamed as the engines roared loudly. All the fans jumped to their feet and leaned forward to view the start.

Aiden jumped on to his seat and leaned against his cousin. He then squinted toward the start line to see the green flag drop and swerve intensely. In unison the cars leaped forward and made the first turn. All drivers seemed to know their positions as they positioned side-to-side and forward to back.

Aiden looked across his seating row and observed his family widen their eyes in utter excitement. His cousin John threw a large smile and tapped Aiden's back. As the cars raced faster in the distant straightaway he could hear the crowd chatter up a storm—they all seemed to exude their exhilaration in unity.

Once the cars approached turn four the lead three cars jetted back and forth until they aligned behind each other. This increased speed awed Aiden as all the cars zoomed through turn four. Suddenly a strong wind gusted and debris flew throughout the seating rows. Aiden brought his hands higher and wrapped them around his ears from the screeching and bellowing sounds.

He then felt someone grab his shoulder . . .

Katie had watched Aiden for a few seconds. She smiled as she noticed him staring off across the street with hazy eyes. She didn't have to imagine the daydream he must be experiencing during his long wait outside—astonishment was evident on his face. She taped his shoulder. "Are you OK?"

Aiden lightly shook his head as he looked back with a smirk.

"I just had an awesome dream. We were at the Daytona 500 and the loud cars were great!" He instantly opened his diary and started to write quickly.

Katie sat down on the step next to him.

"Honey, I believe it's time for you to come inside and at least eat something. You've been sitting out here for more than two hours."

Aiden released a captive look. "Has dad called?"

"No. He didn't call. I tried calling him earlier with no answer."

Aiden gently placed his pen down on the diary and sadly looked into her eyes. The pen rolled off the diary and landed by his feet. Both his legs stretched out completely as he took a deep breath.

"He must be on his way mom. If not he would have called."

Katie felt an internal shake. "We can both go inside and give him another call."

A rush of relief flooded Katie as Aiden blinked his eyes in acceptance. He bent forward, picked-up his pen, then stood to his feet. Katie noticed his jacket unzipped. The temperatures sure do increase quickly this time of year. Given another hour or so Katie knew his jacket would be removed and hanging on the metal railing.

After Katie followed Aiden into the house she closed the door and blinked an eye at her mother. Aiden walked into the dinning room, sat at the table, and without delay opened his diary to keep writing. Nana blinked back with a grin as Katie continued into the dinning room.

"How about breakfast? I can make you some pancakes with bacon."

Aiden diligently kept writing. "OK."

Katie smiled as she gathered all the cooking and food items. By no means did she ever discern herself as a cook she just tried her best to attempt new recipes. Katie didn't mind simple entrees she knew her mother and son would eventually complain about having the same all the time.

Within the past couple years Katie's increased workload hours unfortunately exhausted her cooking time and energy. She never asked Aiden to cook a meal but one day last year he astounded Katie with a finished spaghetti dinner. Granted the spaghetti noodles were stiff and the sauce was cool. This meant Aiden understood his mother's conundrum with work and Katie could see it in his eyes. She felt blessed having him as her son with his helpful actions, many she never asked for.

This astounded Katie and enforced her direction to focus more on Aiden's happiness. That way he would be a sound and joyful adult.

What annoyed Katie about herself the most was her lack of total control in her son's growing years. She knew being a parent was hard and she knew firsthand that being a single parent tended to be harder. She had custody, household responsibility, and financial control, and that also meant Aiden's world was on her shoulders and that sometimes made her feel isolated at one point or another.

Katie respected her family's loyalty and strength towards each other. Her mother was a saint in her eyes along with her four sisters who held each other's backs no matter how difficult or joyful a situation was. Katie certainly felt blessed.

Katie didn't know how she'd managed to be halfway done cooking breakfast after all her internal thinking. Her heart was racing already, and she felt light-headed and dizzy, just wondering why Stewart didn't show after he promised. That was typical Stewart, not thinking of anyone else but himself.

After the breakfast was finished and equally distributed on to three plates Katie called her mother into the dinning room. Aiden was still writing a bunch of words into his diary. Katie handed off the plates on to the table and strayed back into the kitchen to pour herself another coffee. It felt good knowing all three of them would have full stomachs this morning. She then sprung her head back as Nana cleared her throat.

"Can you please pour me another cup?"

Katie flexed her arm carrying the full coffee pot. "I sure can." She then noticed Aiden without a drink. "What would you like to drink?"

Aiden nodded. "I don't care mom."

After she filled Nana's cup Katie headed back into the kitchen and rested the coffee pot on the counter. She then carried a cup and full bottle of orange juice back to the table. Aiden immediately opened the bottle and filled the cup. Katie felt a little strange because she normally filled his cup. Didn't matter though Aiden was still staring at his open diary and cutting his pancakes into small pieces. His attention was in a good place.

A few minutes later everyone adherently ate their food and sipped from their cups. Not many words were spoken as Katie and Nana continuously stared at Aiden. He wrote many words into his diary and never raised his head.

Katie wondered how he felt but didn't want too disturb or halt his writing. He looked devoted, he looked good, but one disturbing thought kept turning over in Katie's mind: How am I going to make Aiden happy for the rest of the weekend?

CHAPTER NINE

Aiden had nothing but time today. Katie thought hard as she finished cleaning the dishes after breakfast. It was a beautiful day, one Aiden could've enjoyed at the amusement park with his father. Typical Stewart. *How can I make Aiden feel better?*

Katie's eyes were filling with tears as she considered many ideas that were important to her feelings.

As Katie placed the last clean plate into the cabinet the phone rang. She answered the phone in a daze, assuming it was Stewart calling to apologize.

"Hello." Katie said nonchalantly as she lighted up a cigarette.

"Good Morning Katie." Her sister Susie said with exciting voice tone.

Katie immediately felt a thousand times better. "Hi Susie. How are things going today?"

"Things are going well. I'm in the area visiting children and will be stopping by your house in a bit to see mom."

"Sounds good. The doors are always open for you."

Katie hung up the phone and smiled. All of her internal frustrations slipped away. Her oldest sister Susie was about to visit and that meant a blissful personality would visit the house and bring joy and laughs. She was renowned by family for her support.

About a half hour later Katie heard this snazzy sounding engine pull into the driveway. She knew that meant Susie arrived in her Porsche 944. Katie's eyes traveled across the bright red car as she stared out the window. That leased car sure did raise many eyebrows but the family loved it.

As Susie stepped out of the vehicle, she grabbed a bag and surprisingly, Chris stepped out of the passenger seat as well. Chris is Katie's other sister Patricia's son. He is the same age as Aiden. Chris has an energetic personality and one Aiden loves to spend time with. The both of them are in the same class and spend many weekends together.

Through the door Susie and Chris hugged Nana and Katie felt the warmth and love when she wrapped her arms around both. Chris then hopped into the dinning room and sat next to Aiden. Susie sat on the couch next to Nana as Katie took a seat on her chair. Susie rummaged through her bags.

"Brought you both some Cider Donuts and Apple Cider. Chris and I just picked them up at Atkins Farm."

Sue is so sweet. She always brings us tasty items. Katie thought as her taste buds glistened in anticipation.

Katie rose to her feet, bent down, and grabbed the two items.

"Can't ever thank you enough big sister. I will put these in the refrigerator for later."

Susie began talking with Nana as Katie stepped through the dinning room and headed into the kitchen. Aiden was talking to Chris about his diary and both had profound facial expressions—one's Katie never seen before. This instantly flowed a great feeling through Katie's thoughts. Her emotions were pinging happiness better than an hour before. She loved her family. Katie then listened as Aiden chatted with Chris.

"So what do you think of this diary?" Aiden asked.

Chris kept his eyes in the diary. "This is so cool buddy. I wish I thought of writing stuff down."

Aiden's eyebrows drooped low as he swallowed. "Do you have many daydreams?"

Chris shot his eyes over to Aiden. "Heck no! I do have many nightmares." Chris chuckled. "When did you start this diary?"

Katie instantly turned her head back into the kitchen, as Aiden looked her way.

"It's my punishment for bad grades. Mom ordered me to write down my daydreams." Aiden leaned forward and lowered his voice. "This punishment is fun."

Chris sat back. "Heck yeah. This definitely looks fun."

Katie suddenly felt her heart beat faster. Several times actually. She was astounded how both of them considered this diary. Both of them discerned this punishment as fun. *What does this mean? Did I actually create a punishment?* Katie thought for a few minutes about all of this. She continued to ponder but maintained herself in high spirits. Only seeing Aiden's emotions and report card in the near future would answer her own questions. She knew that was a certainty.

As Katie kept quiet and headed back into the living room Susie and mom were still exchanging thoughts. When Katie sat back down the both of them stared at her in silence. Katie felt like prey being gawked at by hungry predators.

"What's going on?"

Susie promptly looked at Nana then turned her large eyes towards Katie.

"I have a fun idea for Aiden tonight. You don't have to agree." Susie waved her hand. "I will be heading back to my condominium in Norwich, Connecticut tonight and driving back tomorrow morning for Mother's Day." Susie leaned forward. "I will take Chris and Aiden with me tonight and they will have fun getting away from town for a night. Plus, this will help you get ready for our picnic tomorrow. We are still having that picnic in your back yard, right?" Susie spurned a large smile while blinking her eyes.

Katie felt her jaw drop. She quickly closed her mouth and cleared her throat. "That sounds wonderful. We just have to ask Aiden if he wants to go but I'm sure he will. He loves spending time with you and Chris." Katie then looked away and stared at the wall. "This is great news. Stewart was supposed to take Aiden to the Riverside Park today and never showed." She took a deep breath then leaned forward. "This will make him happy."

Susie immediately stood tall. "I shall ask your son."

As Susie walked into the dinning room Katie looked over at Nana and received a large smile with a special kind of gaze, the kind that made Katie quiver good emotions. Katie then remembered the Mother's Day picnic. She remembered her sister's interaction last week that entailed what everyone would bring for food and chairs. The timeline has always worked well for their events. There was never any formal etiquette or official planning when it came to family events. They were a simple family.

Katie rose to her feet and headed back into the dinning room. As she crossed the doorway she immediately saw the excitement upon Aiden's face. He looked the happiest Katie's seen him look in quite some time. A time she couldn't specifically remember but knew this overnight trip would help quell Stewart's lost promise to his son. She just hoped her sister would save the day.

CHAPTER TEN

Aiden's head flew back against the seat when Auntie Susie stomped on her gas pedal. He loved that! He then thought quickly about how he left on this trip. He packed, said goodbye to his mother and Nana, and won the passenger seat for the trip down to Norwich. Himself and Chris played "Rock, Paper, and Scissors" to determine who would ride shotgun on both rides. Aiden couldn't believe he won the ride down and liked his cousin's friendship. Then suddenly Aiden felt sad, really sad, that his father was not providing his friendship. He took a deep breath and stared out the window.

The weather outside was beautiful. The warmth seemed to peak at the right time. Aiden lowered his window and stuck his arm outside. The breeze flowed so fast and the engine roar peaked. He thought back to his daydream about Daytona and quickly veered into observing the locale environment. Along every red light and stop sign Aiden searched for new sites to take away thoughts of his father.

Once they reached the highway Auntie Susie sped the Porsche into the left lane and Aiden stared out the window as they passed cars. Many drivers stared at the Porsche. He then viewed two kids in the back of a car look at him with excited glances. Aiden then felt a chill that made him feel better, he just didn't know why.

About a half hour later Susie mentioned that she was going to take the next exit and fuel up the Porsche. As Susie elegantly exited the highway she reduced speed and the road bore down to large trees on either side.

When they reached the stop sign Aiden noticed a yellow diamond shaped sign that read "Bear Crossing". The silk-screened sign had a graphic picture of a Black Bear mother and cub. Aiden found the silhouette picture very interesting. He looked both ways not seeing any bears. He did notice a trail that looked tight and not large enough for those bears. This made him wonder how they traveled through that path and crossed the wide two-lane road safely. Of course the mother bear would lead but Aiden just felt that all youths attempted to show their adulthood.

Aiden didn't know about this and not as much as he wanted to. He never researched or learned about animal youths. It was certain that all youths relied on their mothers and only lucky youths had their fathers with them as well.

As Susie pulled into the gas station and turned off the engine Aiden stared forward and the distance became blurry . . .

The weather inside the forest was divine. Maple and many other leaves piled amongst each other. The peaked fall foliage cushioned the path to the front. There were many sounds, ones the cub bear couldn't pinpoint if their distance was close or far. All those sounds were safe natured and all of it echoed within the forest.

The cub felt and heard his long deep breathes that grunted during every forward step. Behind him was a deeper sounding grunt. He turned his head and saw his large mother behind him. She looked happy but tired.

Maybe she felt otherwise as the cub knew she needed something.

"Is everything OK mom?"

"I'm fine my dear. We just need to look for something to eat. It's been a while so please keep your sense of smell open."

"I will mom."

The cub blew a few times through his nose to open his smell. He smelt down low then high. He kept pouncing forward and. The vast amount of smell and sound was amazing, there were so many of both. The cub finally stopped. A sudden sweet smell overwhelmed his nostrils.

The mother turned her attention to the left side of the path as they stood still. She muttered and snorted out loud as the cub sat and raised his torso high. As he looked back he noticed his mother's nostrils flaring open with her eyes closed. The cub was enticed. He followed her actions and began to sense a sweet smell as the wind blew their way. Then a smell of crab apples flowed strong down the path. This excited the cub and his mother. Crab apples were both their favorites. The low branches and vast amount of apples on each tree enticed every Black Bear.

A sudden quick stepping sound alerted the cub and his mother. They both didn't move but stared down the path. It was a deer and that meant delicious meat. The cub glanced at his mother as she shook her head left to right.

"Deer is tasty but will take too much energy to hunt them down. We both smell crab apples and have been craving those for days." Mom started trouncing to the left. "Let's go get some."

The cub followed his mother but watched her slow down to a halt. Just in front of them was a long stonewall.

The wall was five feet high with razor wires on top. The cub stopped next to her and saw her stand tall to view the wall.

Mom opened her mouth releasing drools down her cheeks while her nostrils flickered. "I can see the crab tree and it's just past the wall."

She then looked in both directions and fell back down to four legs. The thick stonewall moved downhill to the right. Mom looked frustrated with an energizing glance as she squinted down the wall.

With a determined pounce mom strutted further down the wall. A prance in her step excited the cub. He followed her quickly and trusted her decision. He never looked at the wall just her rear to keep near. All of a sudden she halted and stared down into a hole in the wall. The hole was broken and rounded. Mom put her paw on the cub's shoulder.

"That hole is too small for me to get through." Mom observed the cub's body. "You can fit through it."

She then stood tall and her large front paws rested on top of the wall as she stared through the wire.

"Perfect! There's a crab tree on the other side of the wall."

The cub looked high and could see the tree's branches exuding over the wall. He got excited knowing how close that tree was. His stomach began to grunt and howl. Hunger was about to be over—the cub thought. He moved closer to where mom was pointing and saw through the hole that was narrow and tight.

As he took a few steps and sniffed the hole all the cub could smell was that the crab apples were near. Just a few feet beyond the wall he saw many apples scattered amongst the grass. He then moved forward and took small steps that flowed with curiosity.

Once he moved into the hole the cub felt the sharp wall scrape his thick fur and skin. He lowered himself to the ground and shuffled his shoulders farther through. More and more shuffles then a sudden end. The cub pushed himself and felt his feet slip through the dirt.

"I'm stuck in the wall mom!"

Mom grunted as she lowered her torso.

"You're not stuck."

The cub suddenly felt a vast amount of power. His mother's paws pushed his buttocks with strength. He lowered his legs more and immediately was free on the other side of the wall. The cub looked back at the wall in amazement.

"I made it mom!"

As the cub shook his upper and lower body parts most of the dirt scattered off his fur. He then stood tall against the wall and suddenly noticed his mother's face. Her nose sniffed through the wires.

"Are you OK?"

"I'm fine. How are you getting over the wall?"

There was silence for a few seconds then mom grunted a little.

"I don't think I can make it over the wall." Another few seconds went by. "How about you gather as many apples as you can and throw some over the wall."

The cub shot a glance up the tree.

With sudden steps, grips, and grabs the cub mounted the tree quickly and set himself along a large branch. He began grabbing several of the apples and tossed them across the wall. Within those throws the cub placed some in his mouth and promptly chewed. It was a single bite followed by a sudden swallow. The crab apples were the perfect size and enticed him to take a sudden swallow. Their sweet and sour taste allured him more and more.

Across the fence the cub peeked to see his mother grab many and chew a lot slower than he was. This made him wonder if he would pay later for eating these apples too fast. He didn't care though. The taste was worth it.

A sudden bark and growl in the distance made the cub drop a few apples. He spun his head and viewed the expanse in the near distance. This red barn with large open doors was across the yard but still close enough to worry.

The cub heard numerous barks. From the shadowed open barn doors two large vicious looking dogs popped their heads out. They crept forward several steps and viewed up in the tree. The cub then felt a moist apple drop from his hands and bounce the ground below him.

The two dogs sped quickly from the barn and barked their way closer. The cub took a few steps down the tree and noticed the dogs were already at the tree trunk. They jumped high along the tree and barked louder with spiteful glances. The cub stepped higher as he whined. His mother taught him to stay protected and that dogs couldn't climb trees only large cats could.

The cub then felt his paws shake and noticed the marks got longer along the tree. His strength weakened as his fear increased.

"Ouch!" The cub yelped as he felt nails scratch his rear end.

That instant fear gave him the energy to rise a bit higher. He couldn't control his shaking and fear that made him feel weak. He looked down and saw the two wicked dogs jump higher. Their faces made the cub feel helpless as he huffed louder and louder.

All of a sudden his mother growled across the fence. She pounced, blew, and slapped the ground. A plaintively load moan in a deep tone sent shivers through the cub. This was the most upset he ever heard his mother.

With deep-throated sounds the cub began to hear loud scratches and thumping as his mother's body climbed the wall. She stood on top and bent forward yelping as the razor wires penetrated her belly. She then hurled herself forward and fell to the ground with a loud thump.

Both dogs took several steps back and looked concerned. Their faces displayed leveling fear shivers, ones the cub never saw before.

Mom stood tall and pushed out her arms wide with a loud growl. The cub stared at his mother for a few seconds then noticed her peak his way.

"Climb down that tree and get through the wall!" She yelled in a verbal tone louder than he ever heard.

The cub released his grips and fell to the bottom of the tree. He felt the pain in his rear but didn't care for his mother was protecting him. As he reached the hole in the wall the cub turned around and noticed the dogs bent lower and glanced at each other with winks. He then noticed blood dripping in front of his mother.

Oh no, the dogs are going to attack! The cub instantly thought.

Both the dogs separated farther from each other and lowered their heads as their teeth enlarged. Mom fell to her feet and grunted with a quick whine.

She must be in pain.

The cub then saw his mother momentarily peek back.

"Push yourself through that wall. I will hold these dogs off."

All of a sudden both the dogs leaped forward at mom. She instantly raised her left paw and hit one dog hard. She flung that dog several feet until it landed with a large whine. The other dog jumped on to mom's back and bit hard down on her neck.

Mom grunted with a painful roar. She looked so brave and strong. These two dogs were large, scary and into this fight.

The cub suddenly felt his chest heave deeply and his heart rate increase. He wanted to listen to mom but something deep inside of him kept him still. A sudden rage engulfed his emotions and the cub jetted forward quickly. He pounced faster and faster before he lowered his head and hit the dog that got back on to his feet. The dog yelped loudly as the cub raised his paws and nails with a fast strike at the dog's body . . .

"Are you OK?" Auntie Susie's voice sounded concerned.

Aiden felt both his shoulders get shook. He turned his head and noticed Chris leaning forward with a smile. A little blurry Aiden jetted his eyelids open and closed until vision was clear. Auntie Susie shot her glances over with smiles.

The Porsche rumbled as Susie shifted into fifth gear and sped faster. They were back on the highway. He must have been out of it for at least a little while. The daydream felt real and he remembered every scene, smell, and emotions. Everything.

Aiden reached below his legs and raised his diary to his lap. He quickly opened the pages and began writing fast. A sudden silence in the car appeared to Aiden. Both Susie and Chris were staring at him with confused facial expressions. He looked down then back up with a smile.

Chris smirked. "I thought you fell asleep. You were quiet sitting up there and didn't contribute to our conversations." Chris slipped back into his seat. "Auntie Susie told a funny story and you missed it."

Susie tapped Aiden's leg a few times. "I knew you were dreaming or thinking of something. You looked cute staring down the road as I peeled away from the gas station." Susie closed her mouth with a smile.

Aiden nodded his head as he wrote quickly into his diary. A sudden feeling of being watched sparked his notice of Chris staring into his diary. The rapid closure of the notebook snapped loudly and sent shivers through Aiden's spine. He then stared out the window with less care about the bothersome questions to be asked.

CHAPTER ELEVEN

Katie awakened early and kissed her mom on this beautiful Mother's Day morning. She also thanked her mother for being who she is, a woman she respected for love and support. Katie then spent a few hours in the kitchen making the deviled eggs and macaroni salad—both these food items were her specialties. Katie was renowned for her picnic food items while all her sisters had their cuisine niches and brought them without requests.

There was a problem with Katie's outdoor grill. She definitely knew it was beyond her knowledge. The week prior she mentioned her grill problem with her co-worker Michael Motyka and he met her that night and fixed her grill. She sure did cherish Michael and his friendship. He just enlivened her thoughts and made her smile. One of the things Katie never mentioned to anyone was how she truly felt for Michael. She thought it best to let things ride because whatever happens will happen.

Katie knew she was always weak in relationships due to her emotions. She just never had any luck when it came to the previous men she dated. There were a few times when she was aggressive and asked men on dates. Those never lasted long. Katie just assumed it was due to her not making good decisions on what men she chose. Ever since that mess she felt it best to relax and let any future dating events just happen. Aiden was her focus and she discerned her thoughts toward that.

Although, Michael has been spurning in Katie's thoughts lately. She has been thinking a lot about him with his blue eyes, stature and beloved personality. Katie tried to mentally list Michael's good and bad. That listing was just too overwhelming on the good side. This scared Katie, she just didn't know why. She felt it best to let him work this relationship magic. She wasn't going to budge.

A sudden ring on the phone startled Katie. She quickly placed the finished deviled eggs into the refrigerator and wiped her hands.

"Hello."

"Good morning and Happy Mother's Day my sister."

Katie smiled. "Happy Mother's Day my loving sister!"

"Your son is happy and we had a great night. The car is packed and we are heading home in a few minutes."

Katie felt her heart rate increase. "Great news! Please drive safe and we all look forward to seeing you."

"See you soon. Love you."

Katie hung up the phone feeling content. Susie was always so profound of a sister, one who sparked smiles on all others. She was the oldest sister in the family and not the alpha most are, she was thoughtful and provided caring support to all the others. Katie loved her greatly for that and said an internal prayer for their journey home today.

As Katie walked into the living room Nana was reading her book and a blanket lay over her legs. Nana looked up with interest.

"Was that Susie?"

"It sure was. They should arrive in an hour or so."

Nana looked up at the clock. "Your other sisters should be arriving shortly as well. It's almost eleven o'clock."

"They sure will and the weather outside is delightful and the sky is clear."

Katie headed back into the kitchen and grabbed utensils and stirred within a large bowl. Her last meal item to finish was the macaroni salad.

A sudden harsh feeling overtook her thoughts. It felt like a sudden piece of lightning struck her in the head. Stewart called last night and it was a late call. He apologized to her about not being able to spend the day with Aiden. Stewart was packing and moving to Virginia. He actually giggled in delight about how he got this new job and how happy he was with the move.

Similar to last night's phone call Katie clenched her hands together. She stirred faster with the macaroni salad and pieces flew all over the counter space and floor. She flung the spoon down harshly and lighted up a cigarette. As Katie leaned back against the counter Nana walked in with a concerned facial expression.

"Is everything OK?"

Katie stood angrily and puffed from her cigarette. She didn't really know how to tell her mother this situation but regardless there was no easier way to explain this mess.

"Stewart called me last night and told me he's moving to Virginia. He apologized for not spending time with Aiden and sounded so cheerful during the entire phone call. That bastard! Who the hell does he think he is?" Tears started to flow from Katie's eyes.

Nana moved closer and wrapped her arms around Katie. A sudden flow of tears wept down Katie's face as she held her mother tightly. This phone call couldn't be worse. Stewart was definitely himself being a man thinking of him and no others. Nana bent back but kept her hands on Katie's shoulders.

"I'm sorry you heard that last night. That is crappy. Just know that I'm here for you and Aiden so no matter what happens or what you need I'm here for both of you."

Katie peaked into her mother's eyes. Her mother was a quiet one who normally didn't discuss emotional matters. She was always there for her family just many felt it best to not vent with her.

"I love you mom."

Nana wiped a few tears from Katie's face. "I love you too my dear."

In the distance, just outside the window, Katie noticed two familiar cars pull in the parking lot. Her sister's Pat and Bonnie arrived just as planned. Several other family members exited their vehicles and handed each other dishes and food items.

Katie sprung her head toward the window and Nana looked back. Nana then stepped back pulled a few tissues and handed them to Katie.

"I will open the door for them and invite them in. I want you to finish the macaroni salad and sprinkle some cold water on your face."

Katie shook her head as Nana walked away. This Mother's Day party was about to begin and Katie suddenly felt her emotions return too joyful instead of rage. This Stewart anger will always be there just not today.

CHAPTER TWELVE

Turning on to Canal Street brought excitement to Aiden. Auntie Susie slowed the Porsche into the company parking lot—all three of them knew the family had arrived and were conversing before the grill was started for the party. Timing was perfect.

Chris opened his door and pulled the front seat open. Aiden snuck out and walked to the rear of the Porsche where Auntie Susie opened the hatch and Chris pulled out the large plastic bottle. Every one of them simultaneously unscrewed the valves on their water guns. Chris filled Susie's, then Aiden's, and filled his own water gun. They all screwed their valves tight and began pumping their pressure valves located under the gun's barrels.

Auntie Susie kept a straight face and blinked with excitement. "Time for us to get back in the vehicle and meet the family."

Aiden and Chris both said at the same time "wicked cool!"

After they all entered the Porsche Auntie Susie started the vehicle and stuck her hand out. Aiden saw Chris slap her hand lightly and that silently ordered him to do the same. Chris looked back with a gigantic smile.

"Let's go get some!"

Auntie Susie slowly crept forward the Porsche, looked both ways, and headed towards the house. Canal Street had no traffic except cars parked on both sides of the street meant caution to any driver.

Auntie Susie clicked the directional signal and slowly turned left into our driveway. The whole family was congregated at the end of the lot where most relaxed on lawn chairs. A tent was erected and had many plastic tables filled with covered food items. Cousin Dan held the grill clicker lighter and walked towards the grill. All the aunts, mom, and Nana sat on folding chairs to the left of the crowd. Many looked back and saw the car creep in closer. They all waved with smiles.

Auntie Susie headed forward and slowed to a stop about twenty feet behind the chairs. She kept her face forward with a smile.

"It's time for our Mother's Day Massacre. Chris, I want you to open the door and let Aiden out before we grab the water guns and attack."

Chris kept his face forward with a grin. "OK."

Simultaneously, the doors opened and both exited very gracefully. Chris kept his arm low under the door window as he clicked the seat forward. Aiden bent onward and got both his legs out while holding the water gun low and below the door window.

Auntie Susie then glanced over as both Chris and Aiden stared at her. Aiden noticed her wink when all three of them jolted away from the doors raised the water guns and started to scream. As they pumped the water away all the aunts and cousins screamed with shock and laughter. Uncle Don jumped to his feet raised his arm over his face and jetted past Aiden. Chris headed directly towards his mother and sister and sprayed them both as they lowered themselves into their chairs.

Aiden loved this joyful event, he saw his mother's eyes larger than ever and felt it best to relieve her. He sprayed her directly in the chest as she screamed in a low tone. All the cousins across the lot giggled so hard some fell off their chairs with their hands on their stomachs.

All of a sudden Aiden heard a creaking sound and looked back. Uncle Don and cousin John headed closer with payback facial expressions. Uncle Don pressed the handle and water flowed from the hose heavily onto Aiden's back. He ran as fast as he could before his cousin Dusty tackled him on the grass. Uncle Don and John got closer and lifted Aiden's pants before shoving the hose in deep.

The water was so cold Aiden instantly felt his goose bumps rise amongst his whole body. The water flowed down his legs and up to his chest. Uncle Don then pulled the hose out and headed toward Chris who was surrounded by his sister Tiffany and cousin Dan. As Uncle Don arrived they performed the same payback on him.

Aiden stood to his feet in laughter and watched as all spread around and giggled at each other. Chris was still screaming with the hose in his pants. Many family members were pointing at Chris as they fell back in laughter.

Auntie Susie then spoke loudly as family members calmed down and most went back to their chairs. "Hello everyone and Happy Mother's Day Massacre!"

The wonderful looks on everybody's faces were perfect. Everyone needed this upturn in their lives and celebrated with conversation and many tasty food dishes for hours.

CHAPTER THIRTEEN

The following week Aiden tried to concentrate on classes and the subjects being taught. He remembered what his mother said last week and how upset she looked inside. She always showed her emotions and that night she just looked tired and went right to the point of having him pay attention in school and not drift away into dreams. He continuously told himself to concentrate but still found his emotions dominating his thoughts.

Monday's classes were confusing. Aiden took notes and read through his schoolbooks grieving about what he didn't understand. He could have asked his teachers questions when those subjects were being taught—he just never did that. Was he too far along in classes to quick learn the subjects? Would he ever catch-up on what was being taught? All this perplexed him as he tried to work all this out.

There were a couple of times, in classes on Tuesday, where he noticed himself drifting off into never ever land. He immediately came back to reality and paid attention to his teachers. That didn't last very long before he went right back to daydreaming or rummaging through all his experiences lately.

Today was Wednesday and Aiden knew he was half way through the week. He stopped himself a couple times and wondered why he viewed it that way. Maybe he didn't want to be there. Maybe he didn't know what to think. His classmates mentioned Wednesday as "Hump Day" and this made Aiden giggle.

He then remembered what his History teacher taught him, a quote from George Santayana: *Those who cannot learn from history are doomed to repeat it.* Most of Aiden's class understood that quote and he continually contemplated that concept because he related that to his dreams. The daydreams he experienced never repeated, every dream was new to him and that energized Aiden to explore those dreams. It's how he viewed things. His diary was more important to him than any other book he had and kept it with him wherever he went.

The school bell rang and Aiden realized he wasn't paying attention to his English teacher—her voice tone was a bit dreary. He shook his head and blew off some steam realizing his thoughts blared out into the middle of nowhere taking his focus away from class.

Good grief.

After the bell rang Aiden walked out the classroom. He opened his locker and noticed Lynette, a girl with a locker beside his, standing beside him. She had this strange look as she stared at him—her mouth was open and her facial glare emanated gossip.

"Did you hear about that guy in our grade who just moved to another town?"

"Which guy?" Aiden said as he closed his locker.

"David. He's that big guy who picks on people."

Aiden immediately recalled all those events where David harassed him in gym classes, school hallways, and food court. Pretty much acted like a bully everywhere he saw him. What Lynette just said sounded intriguing and peaked Aiden's curiosity.

"I hope he never moves back." Aiden said with a straight face.

Lynette flinched her eyebrows then smirked. "He did pick on you didn't he?"

"He was jerk."

Lynette crossed her arms over the books on her chest. "His parents are going through an ugly divorce and David's mother is moving him far away with her. There's something legal in that divorce where his father can never see him again."

Aiden thought for half a second. "Who cares?"

Lynette shook her head. "I just can't imagine not ever seeing my father again. That would be horrible."

A sudden burst of pain struck Aiden's thoughts—it was like a dagger plunged into his heart. He bent his head down trying to understand why he was feeling that way. Was he bearing in mind David's father situation or his own? Aiden just didn't want to think about this grief anymore and forced himself to think of something else. Maybe he could learn some other gossip from Lynette and make himself forget these thoughts.

As he looked up Aiden watched Lynette stride towards another friend to pass this gossip story. He then felt some stuffy air in the corridor around him and knew he needed to step outside for some fresh air.

All of a sudden Aiden's eyes unconsciously got drawn to the right. He noticed Meghan walking his way and chatting with her friend. Time instantly slowed down watching Meghan pace with such a graceful demeanor and smile. Her hair flowed to the left side exposing her silky smooth skin that appeared brighter and more stunning than Aiden ever remembered. Her elegant posture mesmerized him as she passed by him with a cheery glance. Aiden prolonged his stare then instantly wondered why he didn't greet her.

What is wrong with me? I hardly ever say anything to Meghan. Aiden grudgingly thought to himself knowing he thought the world of her. But then he realized Meghan didn't even recognize or notice him as she walked by.

Outside the glass door entrance Aiden saw the school buses drive into the parking lot. It was time to finally end this emotional day and that in its self meant a lot. He traipsed toward the front door feeling tired and run down.

As he stomped up the school bus stairs Aiden didn't pay attention to anybody and just flopped into an empty seat. The springs within those synthetic seats jolted him a few times as he lowered himself and lifted his knees to hold his limp stature. There were several laughs and chatter for the next few minutes, but Aiden just didn't have the energy or concern to listen to any of them. His current thoughts overwhelmed those conversations that he believed were mainly pointless and just passed social time until students were home.

After the school bus door creaked amongst closing the bus rolled forward and jolted over every little pebble and bump along the road. This was one of Aiden's pet peeves with school bus rides and wondered if students would ever get more comfortable and safer public rides. He often thought of those public things and repetitively heard questions from others asking why there were no seat belts on these school buses. The only answers involved lack of money and budgets. Aiden didn't understand that money thing anyway.

The school bus driver abruptly stopped before turning left on to Newton Street. A sudden and loud "POP" shot out of the tailpipe and startled Aiden. He jerked up in his seat and saw that most students on the bus looked around in amazement while others continued their conversations. He then noticed his school bag had dropped to the floor and was sliding back as the bus increased its speed. As he dipped down low and caught the strap, Aiden simultaneously sat back in his seat with frustration. *What an emotional day!*

That sudden loud boom noise annoyed and scared him. He felt his heart rate quadruple in speed as his hands shook atop his legs. As the school bus continued forward Aiden looked out the window and watched the houses whip by.

The internal bus conversations started to increase and Aiden immediately recognized Meghan's voice. He sat taller and viewed over the seat in front of him. Meghan sat with her best friend and laughed with each other as the whole bus jumbled up and down amongst the pot holed streets.

As he took a deep breath and sat back down within his seat Aiden's thoughts continued to fly all over the place. All those thoughts now involved Meghan and how he admired everything about her. His only internal thought problems were that he never could figure out why he felt so much for a girl he hardly knew. He often ignored that problem and continued to dream about her. He knew he was anxious and scared to approach a girl he emotionally felt so much for.

Chapter Fourteen

Katie stared at herself through a blank computer screen, feeling like a stockbroker waiting for the morning bell to ring. She was told from the computer technician that the system crashed last night and was being re-booted. *This is great*, Katie grudgingly thought because she knew all the data that arrived yesterday would have to be sent again. All of the company's offices told her that today's data was most needed for quarterly reports.

Last night was another wide-awake in bed with open eyes night. *Whoopee!* Katie contemplated for a second before taking another sip of coffee. Caffeine was the key to her success and she couldn't imagine not working without it.

Through the office window Katie noticed some shadows moving around the break room. Those shadows looked familiar and normally at this early hour it meant her boss Mr. Sordun, and Michael were getting their coffee ready. Katie waved at Michael when he walked in this morning. Michael tossed a wink back at her and one Katie judged as interesting because that wink had a lot of meaning due to his savvy facial expressions.

It was still early and Michael was the only employee she saw walk through the main door. Mr. Sordun must have entered his side door because he was the only one who kept the key to that lock.

Katie focused back on her screen and saw the light get brighter—that meant several minutes were still needed. She arose out of her chair and headed toward the door. As she opened her office door the two gossipy women from the accounts payable office entered the main entrance. Both those women were dressed to the nines and that made Katie wonder what information or announcement she missed. She let them gabble by her quickly before she followed them a few steps down the hallway.

Inside the break room was Mr. Sordun and Michael. Katie foresaw that correctly. Mr. Sordun was suited up in a plush and expensive suit; he was believed to be traveling to some conference later that afternoon. Michael on the other hand looked tidier than normal with a shaved face, new shirt and tie. Katie immediately wondered if Michael was traveling with Mr. Sordun.

"Good morning gentlemen."

Mr. Sordun and Michael turned their heads in unison. "Good morning Katie."

Katie walked around them and opened the refrigerator for some milk. In her peripheral vision she noticed Michael still staring at her while Mr. Sordun continued to talk about tonight's meeting topics. Katie felt this sudden tingle and instantly stopped to wonder why she was feeling that way.

Meanwhile, Mr. Sordun tapped Michael's shoulder as he briskly headed out of the room. "Both of you have good days."

Michael took a few steps forward with the coffee pot and gracefully filled Katie's cup. They simultaneously opened their mouths then closed them with smiles. Katie quivered when she glanced into Michael's stunning blue eyes—one's that sparkled joyous sensations through Katie every time she saw them. She immediately jolted her head away as she closed the refrigerator door.

"Thanks for the coffee gift." Katie said with a grin.

"You're very welcome. Besides, you made this coffee so I thank you." Michael said while he slid the pot back into the coffee maker. He then leaned back against the counter.

Katie took a few steps closer.

"Are you attending some conference tonight with Mr. Sordun?"

Michael smiled thinly. "Conference?" His eyes then opened wider. "Oh, that conference. No, I'm not going to that upscale event. Only Western Massachusetts CEO's will attend that corporate conference. They all wear political attire and slap each other's backs to make each other feel better. I can only imagine the best actor wins in that event."

Katie giggled as she sipped down her coffee. "You put that event into perfect words." She then dipped her head in salutation.

"What made you think I would attend such an event? I mean I'm just a worker bee like yourself." Michael took a few quick swallows. His face glanced over to the wall without anything on it before returning his eyes. "I've been meaning to ask you . . ."

A sudden BEEP startled both of them. The internal intercom was extremely loud within that break room. After a follow-on click the secretary elegantly cleared her throat.

"Mr. Motyka, you have a call on line two. Mr. Motyka, you have a call on line two."

Michael slipped his stare from the speaker. He raised his eyebrows and shoulders in a slow motion glance returning to Katie's eyes. Katie could tell he wanted to tell her something important she could see it in his posture and a facial expression she's never seen before. Michael was an open-minded man one who always looked calm and never alerted others into confusion.

A hundred emotions played across his face and for a moment Katie was suddenly assured that Michael needed open ears or someone to vent something too. All these new facial expressions sparked Katie to wonder about Michael and his life. Was there something wrong? Did he have a problem he needed to express to someone? Was it work related or personal?

Michael took a deep breath. It was not in his nature to open a conversation and quickly close. But he had a call to answer, a probable call that dealt with corporate contracts and funding.

"Excuse me Katie. I wasn't expecting that call this early, but must take it." Michael tapped his watch. "Gosh that call is early and not expected."

Michael lightly tapped Katie's shoulder. She felt a sudden rush of joyful feelings as curiosity spread quickly through her body.

"It's OK Michael." Katie mentioned while he sped out the door. She jetted to the hallway as Michael limped faster. "You know where I will be all day!"

Michael raised his thumb as he opened another door.

Katie slowly stepped into her office and sat in her chair while crossing her arms close to her chest, as if placing herself into this tight perch that would make all this confusion go away.

She knew there was something different with Michael, a feeling that exhorted a form of content never felt before. This created a form of confusion within Katie, one that inspired many questions. Are there problems with Michael? Did he need someone to voice those too? Why me? Does this mean something? Katie had many sisters that opened to each other for resolutions and concerns about many things.

Katie swallowed and she realized she was nervous. Her extremities shook and felt cold. She couldn't count the number of years she'd fallen for men who never progressed further than romance. A new pattern of loyalty, trust, and respect was Katie's friendship priority; love could follow after all those checks were completed. That was her new belief in relationships and one she was going to stick with. Love will never trump friendship!

Katie then wondered why she had to care so much? She internally devoted herself to Aiden and placed her personal emotions to the side. That was her fidelity in life and she promised herself to never let any other person trouble that.

There was just something about Michael that intrigued her greatly. His personality and manner were perfect in her viewpoint. His devotion and support to his daughter was profound and parallel to Katie's belief. Katie could never dismay his veteran past, one of extreme and violent actions he experienced in Vietnam. She respected his service to his country and the disability he dealt with internally and emotionally.

She didn't quite understand that Michael now had the power to make her happy beyond her wildest dreams. That also meant he had the power to crush her heart . . .

Chapter Fifteen

Several hours passed as Katie inputted data faster than she expected, her professional focus returned quicker than she expected and that meant a successful day ahead. Across the room and still on the phone Julie sat back in her seat and giggled continuously. Julie just seemed to be having a good day with friends or her husband. Julie did spend a lot her time on the phone. There were many past times when Katie had to question Julie's work performance, she just wasn't holding up to the increased data inputting requirements.

Katie went back to data inputting when her office door opened.

Michael. She wondered why she was surprised. Michael daily dropped off paperwork that needed to be stored within our company's system. He was holding a large stack of paper in his hands and had a familiar look upon his face. Katie knew that look. He was up to something. He'd probably spent the morning dealing with a new or existing customer that required much of his time. That could be seen with all the paperwork he had.

He crossed the room and dropped off half his stack on Julie's desk. The look on Julie's face was one of drudgery. She just expressed a look like she was going pick-up something on her desk and throw it.

Michael was at Katie's side in less than a second. He placed the other stack of papers into the inbox, one that over ran the box's perimeter. Katie knew she needed to go back to work and keep inputting data. She just couldn't take her eyes away from Michael.

He pulled a chair closer and sat beside her. "How are you doing today?" he asked.

"Oh, just ducky today. How about you?" Katie replied in a sarcastic tone.

"I don't know how I did it but I landed a contract with one of largest shoe companies in America."

Katie let out a funny little sound that was part laugh, part snort, and part sigh. She immediately questioned herself. What the hell did I just do? Why did I act that way? She knew time was of the essence for explanation. Michael's eyes grew larger. She then put her hands together and placed them on the desk.

"Congratulations and that sounds great!" Katie said before she jabbed her foot into her other leg.

Michael's nostrils grew larger as he lowered his eyes. "I apologize for this morning. That phone call lasted a long time and we worked out the parameters for our contract." His eyes lifted and stared deeply at Katie. "I basically wanted to know if you were available for a dinner." His cheeks formed a darker red blush. "I mean . . ." Michael stuttered. "Would you like to go out on a date?"

Michael lifted his hand to his face; his fingers shook against his forehead as he wiped it. Katie could see him breath deeply and this nervousness grew inside of him. It suddenly became obvious to Katie that Michael had thought about this date for some time. He actually thought of her in similar ways that she thought of him. She could only imagine how nervous she would be if she were the one asking.

Katie then blushed as she lightly tapped his arm. "Of course. I would love to go out on a date with you." She followed that with a smile and a blink of her eye.

Michael quivered with a nervous swallow before he sat back with a smile.

"I will pay of course." Michael's facial tone quickly changed and leaned forward. "I hope you didn't take that the wrong way."

Katie giggled. "Of course I didn't. How can you expect me to pay for a date when you asked?"

Michael laughed hard. His emotional tension was beginning to dwindle.

"I will admit that I'm a wimp when it came to asking you out."

Meghan tilted her head and raised an eyebrow. "You make it sound like I'm a model." She viewed herself from her feet up to her chest as she stood. "I'm just a normal woman in looks but a model behind this rouge." Meghan elegantly lowered herself to her chair then began pointing to her head. "What I have in here will suit you best Mr. Motyka."

Michael swayed his head left to right. "You are too funny Katie."

"That's me Michael, a person who always displays who she is. I don't have the energy to look or acts like someone else."

"Same here." Michael nodded his head.

All of a sudden Katie thought of Aiden and how this date may be a few dates. She quickly drew back all her current thoughts and focused her attention on Aiden. He was her priority. How could she push her personal emotions to the side? That had already been violated in her perspective. Had that violation just happened or was it just now at this moment? Maybe she pushed her belief to the side on this, maybe she had no control over that, and maybe her emotions were taking over her personal belief.

Katie sat there motionless. She then realized Michael was there. There was a moment of silence as Katie tried to compose her words.

"If you don't mind me asking Michael, and I don't mean any harm in this, but can we work out timing for this date? We both are single parents and must assure to each other that our loved ones are being watched by another and are OK."

Michael smiled slowly. "What you're asking Katie makes total sense and I agree." Michael then raised his hand up only displaying index and middle fingers together. "I give you Scouts honor that I will work our kids into our date schedule with you."

Katie then clinched her eyebrows together as she leaned forward. "I like you Michael and find you trust worthy. I'm only sticking to my personal belief that Aiden takes priority in my life. I believe you understand that."

Michael tenderly placed his hand on Katie's shoulder. "Of course I understand that. I'm with you on our kids taking priority in our life." Michael stood tall. "Maybe we can talk more about our date time tomorrow. I will coordinate with Meghan tonight." He began limping closer to the door before he turned his head around. "If I don't see you later, have a good night."

"Good night Michael."

Katie's eyes followed Michael down the hallway with her feelings carrying along with no fear. Something began to build within her—a mounting pressure. Katie didn't know if it was pleasure or excitement, and at that moment she didn't really care which one it was. All she knew was that she was asked out on a date. The man who asked her on a date was her friend and she knew him better than any other man who could have asked her out.

All of a sudden Katie realized Julie was off her phone and staring directly at her. Katie swayed herself and tossed a smile Julie's way. Julie rolled out of her chair and casually paced her way closer. There was this mulish glance that Julie stuck with as she stopped in front of the desk.

"Hey Katie. You are looking mighty happy right now. Did Michael tell you a good joke, or did he ask you out?" Julie leaned in closer.

Katie swallowed feeling too emotional to speak. All she did was nod with slow ease and a smile she couldn't hold back. Julie was a good person but she was a significant member of the company's non-official soap opera club—all they did was gossip about the truth or what they believed was the truth. Katie had to say something.

"Michael asked me out on a date."

Julie's jaw fell open. A look of disbelief echoed amongst her face.

"Congratulations Katie! Looks like you scored well today because Michael is wanted by many ladies in this company."

Katie clinched her eyebrows. "Thanks Julie."

"I'm going to the bathroom and I will be back soon. Think I will also get a soft drink down the hall too. Oh, and maybe freshen up the face, it's been a long day." Julie mentioned quickly before she pounced out the door and sped down the hallway.

Good grief. Katie thought to herself. She knew a sudden gossip train was full steam ahead and to wherever it goes who knows. She didn't care though her day wasn't over yet and she needed to get some more work done. At least that's what she's supposed to do. A glowing sense of excitement dominated her thoughts.

Chapter Sixteen

Aiden sternly sat at the dining room table trying to comprehend his Algebra book, one that made him feel ignorant and guilty. He just couldn't blame his daydreams for his poor grades. At least that's what he thought at the moment. There were many reasons why he just couldn't comprehend math, it didn't make sense too him. He knew adding, subtracting, multiplying, dividing, and many other basic math skills were useful and needed in people's lives, he just couldn't understand why Algebra was needed for a graduation unless everyone was headed towards physics or engineering future.

A sudden flash outside the window spooked Aiden followed by a low-based rumble that shook some windows. It was late May and Aiden knew that meant Summer Solstice was close. Science was a class in school that semi-confused him. He remembered the logical subjects such as environment and biological patterns because he lived and viewed them every day. It was subjects like chemistry, especially Period Tables that listed chemical elements, which confused him due to the vast amount of information he just couldn't remember. Most students memorized those till testing then quickly forgot.

The clock on the wall read 7:50 pm.

Aiden wondered why his mother was still not home. She's been working too many hours and he often wondered if she was OK. He knew her well but missed her greatly. He didn't pronounce that verbally to her often but always held her close to his heart.

The darkness across the house was his next observation. Aiden walked into the living room and turned on a few lamps. As he walked to the front door he heard the porch door open. He first got scared but then knew exactly what to do, he turned on the porch light and viewed through the window.

Mom rattled her keys and swung the door open.

"Good evening my lovely son." Mom said in a soothing and honey-laced tone.

Aiden took a few steps back. "Hi mom."

She stared directly into his eyes. Her opulent glance immediately sent quivers through his body. He rarely saw that passionate look on his mother. It was months maybe years since he saw her appear so ecstatic.

Mom's daily norm was to walk into the house, kiss or touch his skin, and get changed into comfy outfits for the night. She then vented her daily work by either doing the laundry, brewing a cup of coffee, maybe tea, or stepping outside in the back porch to smoke her emotions away.

It just shocked Aiden that mom looked supple and excited. She so elegantly kissed him on the cheek before she swayed into the dining room, dropped her purse, and headed to her bedroom. Something was weird. His mother didn't even look at the mail. It was as if her emotions were somewhere else.

Aiden raised his shoulders in confusion as he stumbled back into the dining room. He then reminisced about many good emotions his mother felt and displayed too him. He compared those joyful looks to smiles pasted upon Disney characters and the happiness they sent to others.

Some music then began to play in mom's bedroom. Aiden knew that song. Mom watched that movie incessantly at home and that theme always stuck in his head. He glanced out the window and thought more. The last thing he would do is stop trying to remember that song. It then dawned on him quickly that the theme was from the 1970's movie Love Story. It was elegant and surreal—mom loved that movie and soundtrack.

This made Aiden wonder why it has been so long since his mother played that soundtrack. He felt his heart beat faster and could feel his neck stiffen. *Did this mean something was happening with mom? She either met a guy or someone that enticed her joy.*

Aiden sat back in his chair as his vision stirred into a blur . . .

Elegantly surreal stars flickered amongst moist vineyards in the distance while up close was an elegant precious stone renaissance village with pronounced clay roof tiles. A warm breeze flowed through the 16th century Italian genre themed village.

Aiden floated in the air as he viewed all the scenery and this made him wonder because he never consciously controlled a daydream before. He literally felt weightless as he hovered above the ground to view from the air. Aiden thought for a few seconds before he motioned himself several feet to his left. *Holy Cow!* He followed this curiosity by leaning forward and sticking his arm straight ahead of himself. *So this is what Superman feels like when he fly's!* Excitement burst Aiden into speed as he easily maneuvered himself amongst the stone laced streets.

Suddenly a well-defined feeling of family overwhelmed Aiden. It was as if this village was familiar to him. He somehow knew all the community and its residences as if he lived there.

Aiden then focused on this quaint village portion of town, one where a renaissance male statue sat above a fountain that flowed continuously into a water pool. All the surrounding buildings were dark except for this lighted balcony that rested on the top floor to this affluent building. Aiden felt this sudden pull closer where he noticed a Marble laced flooring topped with pillared marble railings that swept across an oval shaped balcony.

Seconds passed. Many of them actually as Aiden stayed in place with this appointed feeling that kept his focus. Each second was filled with silence except for a distant quaint bird chirp and chirp some more.

An attractive woman then sauntered on to the balcony. She wore a silky laced gown fitted to her waist with a full skirt flowing below. A sudden shine flickered from her collar-like necklace surrounded by jeweled pins and stones. The woman then looked off the balcony to her left and right. Her braided hair was puffed over her ears and drawn back into a wrapped twist at the nape.

She looked familiar to Aiden and he just didn't know why. *Who is she?* He kept asking himself. His vision hovered closer as he flowed to the front of the balcony.

Oh god! Aiden recognized his mother's face. Her skin was lightly colored and whiter than normal with make-up all over her face.

Why is mom here in this village? Aiden's heart raced with tingly feelings jetting through his veins. His mother's face displayed this graceful stare. It was as if she was searching for someone. She was expecting to see someone but it sure wasn't Aiden. He was just in front of her and this was only a daydream.

Mom's stare suddenly was docile. She took a deep breath and her eyes grew larger. She then placed her hands on the balcony and leaned forward.

"O Stewart, Stewart! Wherefore art thou Stewart?"

Stewart? That's dad's name. Aiden abruptly felt confused.

He then heard a few steps below. Aiden looked down and saw this man wearing tights for pants and a maroon colored linen renaissance shirt with trumpet sleeves that were tight on the upper arm and flared below. This man tottered forward from the shadowy darkness and into the lighted side of the fountain. His long sleek hair shined as his straight legs trounced ahead.

"I am here my love." The man lowered to his knee and looked emotionally upward towards mom. "The trinkets of love show brightly between us."

Aiden flinched his eyes tightly and stared deep. *That's dad!* Aiden swallowed hard and felt his joy increase. Mom and dad were together again! Aiden looked back at mom. She placed an extended hand above her eyes.

"Why fore art though living so far away from me?"

Dad's voice dwindled in response. "I go where life is best for both of us my dear."

"Our sacred son. Our son needs both of us."

Mom's eyes became damp. Her lips started to tremble.

A sudden abrupt and louder trumpet sounded. But it wasn't a trumpet it was a saxophone. In addition, a rapid sounding scream increased in volume. This greatly confused Aiden as he experienced a quick ruckus. Something was getter closer . . .

Aiden leaned back on the chair and viewed mom in the kitchen. She poured some screaming hot water into her teacup. He loudly cleared his throat and grunted. Mom blinked a surprised look his way as she suddenly stopped whistling to herself.

"Is everything OK?" Mom's eyebrows clinched together.

Aiden twisted himself sideways in the chair. For a few seconds he compiled his thoughts from the sudden daydream he witnessed. It was a daydream like no others— he controlled his views while witnessing the dream.

"I just had the most strange daydream mom or something that seemed like one."

Mom placed her spoon into the sink and strolled closer. She pulled out the nearest chair and lightly sat. Aiden stared as the steam flowed from the teacup. Mom cordially placed her hand upon his arm.

"Do you want to tell me about your daydream? It's OK if you don't. No pressure."

"Of course." Aiden said while considering what he was about to say might anger mom or his own self. He reminisced past conversations where he told his mother what he thought she wanted to hear; all those fictional stories that meant nothing at all. Mom saw right through those and never got angry she just shook her head and called his bluff.

Aiden tapped mom's hand. "This daydream looked like a Romeo & Juliet movie. The scene was very Italy like or somewhere like that, it just looked pretty cool and real. I could smell the breezes and you were dressed so elegantly." He chuckled with a grin. "Your dress looked silky and your hair was braided. You basically looked rich and definitely a pretty woman."

"Wow! Wish we could videotape your daydreams." Mom sat back and sipped her tea with a grin.

Aiden then felt serious. He really didn't know another way to express this. "You were calling for dad from that balcony. Dad arrived and was dressed like the past. He actually looked funny being dressed in tights." Aiden spurted a small grin. "You could hear dad say something about himself living far away and for some reason you couldn't see him."

Mom's face instantly seemed frightened and cold. It was as if she was shocked by something. Aiden leaned forward.

"Are you OK mom?"

Mom inhaled a deep breath. "I'm so sorry for not telling you earlier. You just reminded me of something I haven't told you yet." Mom's facial expression mirrored an internal beating. "I apologize."

Aiden shot back in his chair. He felt like some bully at school, or down the street, just punched his heart. Mom then leaned closer.

"Your father called me the other day and said he's moving to Virginia for a job."

Aiden's nose slowly twisted in sneer. A shivering coldness trounced through his innards creating these large goose bumps, ones that pulsed and made him shake. He felt as though he was sitting near the North Pole.

"Why would dad do that without telling me or saying goodbye? Is that why dad didn't show last week? He was moving and didn't care to tell me." Aiden voiced louder than normal.

"I truly don't know why he didn't stop by here to see you or talk with you about this. I wished I had those answers." Mom started to shed tears. "I apologize for not letting you know sooner."

The goose bumps immediately flattened away as hot blood flowed through Aiden's veins. He stood out of his chair and trounced down to his room. At the doorway he quickly halted. He heard a squeal and one he never heard before. He poked backwards and saw mom's head shake between her crossed arms on the table. It was the loudest cry he ever heard from his mother.

Aiden took a deep breath. He couldn't explain all this anger and sudden hatred he was feeling. It darted away into guilt with another person's emotions out pacing his own emotions. But this was mom the woman who meant the world too him. His best friend and someone he trusted more than anyone else on this planet.

Aiden slowly returned to the dining room table. He couldn't sit. He couldn't talk. His emotions over took his actions. He bent down and wrapped his arms around his mother's waist. She rolled off the chair and sat on the floor wrapping her arms around him. They hugged and consoled each other for hours.

Chapter Seventeen

It was Saturday morning.

Aiden immediately stretched his legs before opening his eyes. The sunlight shot through the window as he yawned himself awake. He shot his head over to view the clock and 7:50 digitally displayed dimmer than normal, that meant he awakened just in time to watch his favorite cartoon. He sat vertical and stretched his arms over his head taking a deep breath.

The Looney Tunes cartoon was about to begin and Aiden loathed missing an episode. He instantly planned out his morning rituals: A dressing in comfy pants, a bathroom visit, a glass full of juice, and cranking on the television—one that took a few minutes to warm-up. Nothing was going to get in his ritual way, nothing at all. That was his Saturday morning center of attention and he intensely followed that path to happiness.

As he crept into the living room, with his chilled glass of juice, he nonchalantly sat on the couch. He whipped his right hand to grab the remote control from the end table—a location where the controller was serendipitously kept. On the end table was a faded color shaped like the remote control to prove that.

All of sudden the television connection turned off. Aiden raised his eyebrow and grunted loudly. A break in

Looney Tunes felt like a nightmare and especially being fully awake and paying attention. He stared at the fuzzy screen for a few seconds before he sauntered his vision across the living room. The furniture and decorations within the living room were arranged in a simple manner: green leafed vases along the floor, wood framed pictures along the walls, and standard furniture aligned against the walls. Only a long glass coffee table obstructed direct movements across the living room. The carpet was thin and during colder seasons the wood-flooring base underneath creaked loudly, especially wearing heavier shoes. *Boring!* Aiden thought quickly passing the time.

Once the television connection reappeared Aiden quickly stared back at the cartoon characters he loved the most. He then, within a nanosecond, found his emotions shifting back to a surreal spirit. Aiden's multi event thinking was all he knew or recalled and those thoughts were viewed under his control.

For the better part of an hour Aiden murmured the character's wording to the cartoons he remembered distinctly. His breath and heart rate accelerated in his most favored comical episodes, even the ones he saw multiple times. It meant so much to view and experience anything that made him feel that way. Granted, it was only a cartoon that enhanced his personal delights.

Tedious minutes passed during commercials. It seemed as though commercial timing grew longer each week and louder to say the least. Aiden knew it best to hit the mute button on the remote controller. Commercials didn't mean much at all except for the new toys, Atari games, sports equipment, and especially the tasty new meals and candy. Aiden was normal and fell into the commercial market syndromes of success for children begging their parents to buy whatever it was that excited them.

The floor then creaked and alerted Aiden. He raised his head up and shot his eyes back and forth. Mom was awake! She normally awakened sooner but after their emotional events last night he fully understood her late sleep. He then wondered how mom's emotions would be this morning. He knew it best to hesitate his predictions because most times he was wrong. He expected mom to be quiet because she normally was during her next day recovery from sordid emotions.

Her steps got closer into the kitchen. Aiden held the remote controller in his hand and left the mute on. He then heard mom yawn loudly before she opened the coffee maker. "Oh!" Mom halted her yawn and then coughed a bit. It sounded like a surprise or, even better, excitement. A click then sounded and that meant the coffee maker was turned on. The gurgle and bubbling sounds began the brew.

Mom poked her head into the living room.

"Good morning pumpkin and thank you for preparing the coffee."

Aiden blasted a wide closed lip smile. "Good morning mom. I hope you slept well last night?"

Mom then rubbed her closed eyelids away. Another short yawn slowly happened as she moved closer and kissed him on the cheek. A kiss meant the world to Aiden because it instantly told his innards that mom was in a good mood.

Last night's emotional situation between the both of them was harsh. Aiden still felt the frustration and pain, he just couldn't fully understand why it was happening but did know who was responsible . . . his father. What a confusing man his father was, someone Aiden could never figure out or understand. Many told him that his father was an internal man and that made no sense to him. What is an internal man? Was that a man who lived like a hermit and never interacted with many others? Mom always told Aiden that his father did love him. His father always verbally expressed that over the phone or in person but hardly ever physically displayed his wordings. He just called and spoke from wherever he was.

Please stop thinking. Aiden pronounced to himself. This whole round a bout thinking mess just tired him greatly. Looney Tunes was running and he already missed several cartoons. Aiden pressed the mute button again and smiled.

Pepe Le Pew was weaving his rear end closer and closer to this female cat with a clothing line clip squeezing her nose shut as she got backed into a corner. Pepe's French accent was strong. *"One of the mysteries of my life is why a woman runs away when all she really wishes is to be captured."* Pepe Le Pew snuck closer and wrapped his arms around the female cat that lifted her head in fear. Pepe romantically stared into her eyes. *"It may be possible to be too attractive."* He peeked into a mirrored window and stroked his hair back. He then blinked into the female cat's wide-open and scared eyes. *"Why is it when a man is captured by a woman all we wish to do is get away?"* The female cat sucked in her belly and snuck through Pepe's arms. She then burst away quickly.

Aiden chuckled as that episode finished and went to commercial. He reached over and grabbed the empty glass before he headed into the kitchen where mom scrambled eggs in a bowl while the frying pan was being heated.

Aiden thought quickly. *Why is mom making breakfast so early?* She normally drank her coffee and awakened a bit more before she ate anything. Even more discerning to Aiden was that they took turns daily and shared the weekend breakfast cooking. Mom made the last weekend breakfast and that normally meant today was his turn.

Was this a relief mechanism for mom? She did look emotionally horrid last night. Mom's normal relief for her bad days at work was performing little projects around the house. Her silence and not sharing frustrations always confused Aiden. It did let him know when she was in a good mood or not. Silence was certainly not a virtue to Aiden when it came to his mother. He respected his mother's personality and wished she shared her troubles with others just not himself.

Mom finished cooking the eggs and tossed the toasted bread on to the plates. She placed both plates on the dining room table and sat down in her seat with ease. Aiden couldn't figure out which one it was but a look of nostalgia or commitment mirrored off mom's straight stature as she ate. She did look relaxed because her shoulders held low and her eyes gazed out the window. Aiden sat in his chair as his mother puckered her lips.

"I'm sorry Aiden. I meant to tell you last night but we both got overwhelmed with emotions." Mom stared into his eyes. "Nana will be here around eleven thirty to pick you up and bring you to Mont Marie for her afternoon shift. She will then bring you out to eat tonight and spend the night here with us."

Aiden felt his mouth drop wide open. "Is everything OK?"

"Of course Pumpkin." Mom blinked a good feeling. "Your mother has a date today and besides I told you last week about you spending the day with Nana."

Aiden widened his eyes. "A date?" He then leaned forward. "With who?"

"Michael from work asked me this week and I finally said yes."

Aiden remembered meeting Michael at mother's work. He rendered a professional and down to earth approach when Aiden met him. They joked about many cartoons and sporting events, especially the New England Patriots that Mom and Aiden watched religiously every year. Michael just seemed like a nice guy.

Aiden felt a sudden need to view Michael further because this guy was going to date his mother. Was that necessary because his mom hasn't dated anyone in quiet some time? Mom then tilted her head.

"I need your opinion Aiden. I know you've met Michael and said good things about him. We just need to both agree on this. We shared the same blood, fluid, food, and oxygen for nine months before we were one in the same. We got it and we get it together. I hope you understand that?"

Aiden did feel his mother's joy and excitement. He sat back in his chair and pondered this whole situation. Seconds passed before he lowered his eyes and placed both his hands on the table.

Aiden smirked. "Are you going anywhere fun?"

"Hope so, Michael is keeping it a secret but did say I would have fun."

CHAPTER EIGHTEEN

Nana's red convertible was parked in the lot when Aiden heard the front door open. She whistled her way in and looked great. Nana wore her hazel colored chino pants, a thin cotton shirt, an orange and black tiger mascot labeled windbreaker, and sneakers. Nana certainly knew how to dress comfortably for work.

Aiden stood to his feet. "Hi Nana."

"Hello there. How are feeling today?"

"Good."

Nana raised her hands to her hips. "Are you ready to visit Sister Gervais today? She's been asking about you these past two weeks. You visiting her today will make her happy." She then smirked a grin.

A speedy rush of adrenaline shot through Aiden once he heard Nana mention Sister Gervais. She was by far the most profound and respected woman he ever met. He shivered with abrupt attention every time they talked and he remembered every word she spoke. Nana tapped Aiden's shoulders.

"I'll be right back."

Aiden then remembered. "But wait Nana. Did you finish the quilt for Sister Gervais?"

Nana smiled with crows-feet wrinkles at the sides of her sparkling eyes. "I sure did and it's laden with lots of orange yarn. I'll show it too you when we get to Mont Marie."

Nana then headed into the dining room where she talked with Mom. Aiden sat pleasantly on the recliner chair whipping his legs in the air and whistling Down Under by Men at Work song.

Aiden then sat up straight and started looking around. The diary was nowhere in sight. It was as if he was nude in public, at least that's how it felt too him. His head spun in circles as he looked around the living room. He then tapped his pants and shirt with knowing the diary couldn't fit in either.

Aiden stood to his feet and quickly trounced towards his bedroom.

Both Nana and mom were discussing something. They then silenced once both noticed him flying through the dining room. As he entered his bedroom he rummaged through his bed sheets then opened all his dresser drawers. Nothing. *Wow!* Aiden thought too himself because he noticed his lower lip start to tremble. That diary meant more too him than he thought.

He jetted back down the hallway and halted in the dining room. Mom and Nana stared with questionable looks. Mom had her head erect with slightly raised eyebrows.

"Is everything OK? Do you need something?

Aiden quickly responded. "I can't find my diary."

Mom looked down and tapped the diary that lay closed on the table. She scooped it up and held it out with a stiff-arm. Aiden took a few steps as he focused on the diary. All these emotions he felt at this moment were more than he could comprehend. This uncertain location of the diary stimulated this feeling that felt like he was being stomped on or rolled over.

"Thanks." Aiden said as he remembered leaving the diary on the table before he crashed in bed last night. Oh boy, another emotional moment that overtakes his thoughts. *Good grief*! Aiden pondered.

Nana and mom both stood and gave each other a long hug. Nana held her face with both hands and gave her a large smooch before tapping her cheek with a grin. She then glanced towards Aiden.

"You ready big boy?"

Aiden raised his eyebrows and tilted his head forward. "Big Boy! Are you taking me there for dinner Nana?"

Nana chuckled with a smirk as she headed toward the front door. "And away we go!"

Aiden snuck in behind Nana and followed her out the door.

Once they both sat in the red convertible, Nana looked over and mentioned the warming breeze. She released the roof lever and watched the top trickle back. Aiden jumped out of the car and ran back, folding the top into its place.

"It's locked Nana!"

"Let's go for the beauty ride." Nana said as she backed the car and headed on to the street.

The weather for that ride was extraordinary. The warm sunshine combined with warmer than normal breezes brought comfort to Aiden as they looped around the rotary and headed for the Muller Bridge. The Connecticut River shined delightfully as the water was rough and splashed within the breeze. Above the river side tree line were birds that swooped low and high as if they were radar locked to fish in the river.

Aiden sat back in his seat and shot a glance towards Nana's happy face. She loved this car and one she dreamed about her whole life. She drove this convertible all over town and especially during the warmer seasons. Her face looked like a smiling statue as she drove. Her focus was the road and she always stayed alert as to traffic and the roads. The only time she spoke or looked around was when the car was stopped or halted. That amazed Aiden as he sat back and enjoyed the wind flow through his skin.

CHAPTER NINETEEN

When Nana and Aiden drove into Mont Marie parking lot she pulled around the front entrance that led to the rear lot. There is this brick and concrete blended wall that looked almost ebony in color. The middle portion of the building had a taller portion where the glass entrance was ground level and delightfully colored metal cross that rose above the roof. It was a profound building in a location hardly visited by most patrons, friends, and relatives. There were retirement convents scattered throughout Western Massachusetts but Mont Marie was the Health Care Center for all Sisters of St. Joseph of Springfield within the region.

Once she parked the car around the back lot Nana lightly tapped Aiden's knee.

"Are you ready?"

Aiden smiled with parted lips. "I'm ready."

"Let's go."

Aiden followed Nana into the lower back entrance, one that had thick metal doors. Once they entered Nana walked along the shinned floors surrounded by concrete walls. Above the flooring were exposed air and water shafts that ran the entire way. It looked similar to a cobweb just not for spiders. He then followed Nana into her break room, one that had basic chairs with small bookshelves that were overloaded with romantic novels. To the right side was a basic refrigerator, one that Nana placed her lunch bag into.

Nana then headed to the other side of the room and opened her locker. Those lockers were thin, long, and seemed to look rusty to say the least. Nana placed her coat and purse into the locker than slowly closed that locker and spun the wheel.

"It's time for me to bring you up to Sister Gervais' room." Nana winked. "You ready?"

"Sure."

Aiden followed Nana down the hallway and then up the concrete stairs to the main level. As soon the stairway door opened he took in a barrage of sights and smells. The main hallway had smooth wooden floors in the atrium that transferred to concrete flooring between the two medical wings. The atrium's floor-to-ceiling stained and religiously decorated windows were amazing. They sparkled as the sun shot through the courtyard.

Aiden couldn't explain the smell that encompassed the atrium for it was similar to a church smell of wax and various scents. That immediately placed him in wonderment. It amazed him how such a panorama of decorations and smells could take over his feelings. He just wasn't sure what those feelings were and of course never talked about them. He just wasn't sure if those feelings were sacred or not.

Nana continued walking down the left wing and Aiden caught up to her. Most of the hospital room doors were open. He knew better than to peek into all of them but he felt drawn to look out of curiosity. Several of the rooms were empty mainly due to timing. It was divine hour and that meant the Sister's read through psalms and scriptures, held a Mass, followed by a rosary.

Sisters sure do have full days. Aiden pondered.

As they got closer to her room Aiden smiled to all the Nuns as he passed them. What amazed him was how sharp their robes looked and how shined their shoes were. They all wore black colored habits while some flowed long in the back and others shorter. Nana then slowed down and knocked lightly on an open door.

"Hello Sister. It's Dorothy and my grandson Aiden."

Aiden followed Nana in but strode with closed fists and stiff legs. He almost felt like a soldier and just couldn't explain why his stature was so stiff. Sister Gervais' face colored quickly, her cheeks got redder and her facial expression glowed with joy.

"Good afternoon Aiden and Dorothy. It's great to see you both."

Sister Gervais slowly placed her book on the table and leaned forward. Nana quickly raised her arm.

"It's OK Sister, please stay seated."

"Oh, alright." Sister Gervais gently sat back.

Nana opened her plastic bag and pulled out a folded quilt—one that was imbedded with orange colors. As she unfolded the quilt Nana winked as she gently placed it at the foot of the bed. Sister Gervais' mouth dropped wide open as she consequently lowered her chin.

"That's beautiful Dorothy and I thank you greatly."

Nana pointed at Aiden. "You can thank Aiden. He's the one who reminded me of your favorite color."

"You both are so sweet. God bless you."

Nana spun around and tapped his shoulder. "Alright Aiden. I have to go to work. Are you OK with being with Sister Gervais for a few hours?"

Aiden blinked faster. "Of course Nana."

"I'll chat with you later Sister. Hope you both have fun." Nana said as she left the room.

Aiden didn't know what to say or do. He did feel comfortable. It's just that he didn't know how to start a conversation with the Sister who still grinned at her quilt. Sister Gervais then opened her hand and tapped the end of the bed.

"Please have a seat Aiden."

Aiden sat on the firm bed and bounced a little. That bed was by far the stiffest mattress he ever experienced. The Sister then took a sip of water from her glass. Aiden noticed that her hand shook significantly and spilled some of the water upon herself. He spun his head and noticed a folded towel in her open cabinets. When he grabbed the towel and handed it to Sister Gervais, he wondered if everything was all right with her. He didn't remember her shaking the last time he met with her. But then again he didn't know why she was in this medical facility.

Sister Gervais giggled as she tapped the towel along her robe. She then looked up at Aiden. "How are things going at school?"

Aiden hesitated for a few seconds before he responded. He wasn't sure how Sister Gervais would take the truth as he somehow knew he wouldn't feel good if he didn't tell the truth.

"It's not going well. My latest report card had bad grades. I did get a 'B' in History class." Aiden's forehead wrinkled.

Sister Gervais sat motionless for a second then pulled the book back into her lap. She looked down and raised the front cover. "Have you read this book?"

Aiden squinted, as he looked closer. This was a History textbook. *Wait a minute.* That textbook was the one he read last semester. Sister Gervais was the last person he expected to be holding that textbook.

She glanced with a smirk. "Did you know that I was a teacher at Cathedral High School? I taught there for many years."

Aiden's eyes were wide open. "I didn't know that Sister."

"Is this the current textbook you're using?"

"It is the same one."

Sister opened the textbook to a page she had a sticker on. She then mumbled to herself. "These dates and annotations are wrong. This paragraph's verbiage is too political based."

Aiden bent forward to hear her better. Sister Gervais closed the textbook quickly and shot a stare at him. Her voice tone was serene and tranquil and that kept Aiden's attention.

"It's not about the authors who write these school books specifically it's also about the school administrators who accept and purchase them. They're both at fault in regards to this textbook."

Aiden raised his eyebrow at Sister. "I'm sorry Sister but I don't know what you're saying."

"That's all right Aiden. I'm just speaking as a retired teacher." Sister Gervais then placed the textbook back on the table. She pointed her finger to Aiden's side. He looked and realized what she pointed at.

"This is my daydreamer diary."

Sister opened her eyes larger. "Excuse me."

"It's my punishment for poor grades this past semester." Aiden then hesitated. He didn't want to bore Sister Gervais with all this mumbo jumbo about his daydreaming. He knew it best to tell the truth. "My mother told me to write down all these daydreams because I wasn't paying attention in class."

Sister Gervais displayed an inquisitive look. "So tell me Aiden what are you paying attention to? What are you thinking about?"

"That's just it Sister, I'm not paying attention because other thoughts take over current ones." Aiden then halted for few seconds. He wondered if what he was saying was actually the reason. But then again what was the reason? "I'm just confused about everything." Aiden swallowed hard in disgust.

Sister Gervais then leaned forward and tapped his leg. "There's always a reason for what people do whether they realize it or not. As for daydreaming I must tell you that I'm no expert on this subject but will provide you my opinion. The negative side I've noticed from students who daydreamed is that most of them did this at the wrong time when they should have been paying attention in class. It basically prevents a student from learning a subject or finishing homework on time." She tapped his leg again. "Think of it as a turtle who is slow and vulnerable to many predators, it subconsciously knows its defense and hides in its shell."

Aiden quickly noticed his eyes grow larger and his heart rate increase. What Sister Gervais just mentioned about the turtle was surprising. He dreamt about a turtle in one of his daydreams. He was hooked in by what she was mentioning. Sister then smiled.

"Your daydreams are indeed better than reality. By indulging in those wonderful thoughts you become unmindful of your situation and that's why you daydream. I've noticed this with many students I've taught in the past where they isolate themselves from their hardships and confusion. It's just a way they dealt with their problems. I also learned that daydreaming could be positive because it can enhance a child's imagination and creativity." Sister Gervais winked. "I hope that makes sense too you?"

Aiden felt amazed and sort of excited. He didn't understand every word Sister Gervais spoke with but he sure understood her point in that he was daydreaming for a reason. What that reason was, well that was still confusing . . .

CHAPTER TWENTY

Katie was excited as Michael led her down Main Street in Northampton. He picked her up early in the afternoon and surprised her with a shopping event. The weather outside was sunny and warm and that meant great timing to walk through the shopping district, one that encompassed several distinct categories of stores and boutiques.

When they first arrived Michael took her to Fitzwilly's restaurant for lunch. Somehow Michael knew because that restaurant was Katie's favorite place for lunch with its enjoyable decor and brick laden walls. They both had French onion soup with cheese and crackers. Plus a full bottle of Pinot Noir wine that lowered any personal walls Katie might have raised. They talked about nothing with both of them having time to share relaxation and of course Michael joked away a plethora of his laughter creations.

Katie was comfortable and achieved blissfulness. It was as if all her worries were taken away for the day because she originally thought of thanking Michael. She did notice his stance, his facial happiness, and overall ease. Michael was having the same sanctuary day as Katie. This get away for the day with some intriguing, down to earth, and friendly companionship meant their focus was upon each other and nothing else. The hardships and duties in life were yesterday and tomorrow just not today.

While in some of the shops, Katie acquired a few unique trinkets and pieces of jewelry. Michael didn't shop much but had to at least purchase this lovely piece of artwork that halted him for several minutes as he stared deeply into a sunrise off the shores of Long Sands in York Beach, Maine. That painting was hand painted with exquisite oils. The artist was in the store that day and Michael brought Katie over to talk with him. This man was mister 'Artsy Fartsy' to say the least. His personality was laden with surreal minded outlooks. Katie immediately knew this by the adverbs and pronouns compiled within his conversation about his visions and reasons for talent.

After a casual walk back to the car Katie wondered where they were heading to next. Michael kept their day of fun locations a secret. Katie enjoyed that. This envy of unknown sites and directions into obliviousness kept her excited.

Michael drove north on Interstate 91 then exited west on Route 2. This sparked excitement in Katie knowing they were headed for the Mohawk Trail. She remembered several visits along that trail it's just been a while since her last journey.

The signs and Mohawk decorated symbols began to appear along the road. Katie then noticed the rocky and wooded sides to the road that induced a feeling of joy. She loved sights and landscapes. A little further Michael started to slow down. He took an exit and twisted along a two-lane entranceway to Savoy Mountain State Forest. As they came to a halt Michael asked Katie if her feet were ready for a small hike. Katie pondered for a second and gave a thumbs-up knowing her shoes were comfortable enough for a walk.

As they stepped through the scenic wooded trails an area opened up quickly with such visual delight. The sign read "Bog Pond Trail" and that pond was quaint in nature with lily pads engulfing the lakeside. Within the pond floated bog islands that were sized small and large. Katie heard some frogs croaking in the distance followed by croaks that sounded closer. It was a frog concert with groups croaking in musical themes. Katie relaxed her legs and closed her eyes to listen for a few minutes.

Michael then touched and rubbed his fingers along Katie's hand. She instantly felt a shiver that flew throughout her body. She opened her eyes and noticed his blinks and head nods as he directed her back to the trail and into the car.

Katie entered blissfulness. These little moments in her life meant more to her than anything else. Everyday she would halt her activities for seconds, maybe minutes, and take in sights and sounds for the day. Life was a gift in Katie's eyes. There were many people who flew by in life not observing its offerings. There was no way Katie would squelch her belief. Life is short and life is an event that must be captured whenever possible.

Michael drove at a slow speed so both of them could take in the lovely scenic pathway they strode through. The next sign was for Shelburne Falls and that deeply enticed Katie's emotions. She didn't want to contemplate where they were going. She held back her prediction. Oh, its too late, Michael parked in a lot near the Bridge of Flowers. Before Michael turned off the engine Katie stared into his eyes and sparked a gigantic smile. This was her favorite scenic site and one she hasn't visited in what seemed to be a millennium for her.

Katie knew there were hundreds of different flower varieties laden amongst the railings along this thin trolley bridge. This bridge ran across the Deerfield River between the towns of Shelburne and Buckland. Its length is several hundred feet with a five arch ivory-colored concrete span with thin-railed linings.

As Katie and Michael moseyed closer to the bridge there were only a few families and couples that occupied the thin walkway. Katie immediately felt peaceful seeing the purple, white, orange, and yellow flowers stick out like a beautiful thumb. The scents of loveliness flowed like a waterfall through her nostrils. Michael grabbed her hand and Katie clenched his tightly.

There were minutes upon minutes going by as they strolled along the walkway. Katie was lost in flower land and tried to suck in all the scents and sights. There were great things to see along the Deerfield River as Katie focused on the flowers. This tremendous occasion lighted a flame of romance. Michael was the best guy for who he was and also for where he was bringing her. Katie stopped cold. She looked deep into Michael's eyes and thanked him. Michael began to raise his hand before Katie jumped forward and planted a lingeringly kiss upon his lips. This sparkle of happiness exhumed from his facial expressions. A titter and a tatter then led to a glow of redness along his cheeks followed by a deep breath before he gave her a gentle hug.

CHAPTER TWENTY-ONE

Aiden had a peaceful conversation with Sister Gervais. He didn't know why but his respect increased just being near her presence. Her joyous personality sparkled beyond her soft and slow verbal tones. He saw directly into her persona, one that boosted his attention for more and more conversation. He looked up at the clock and realized its been two hours. He then looked at the table and noticed her glass was empty.

"Sister, can I get you more water?"

She coughed low and slow. "Please. My throat is a little dry and sore."

"OK."

Aiden picked-up the cup and headed into the hallway looking in both directions. A nurse station was close and so was a bathroom but no water fountain visually stuck out along the walls. He walked closer to the nurse station and saw this woman dressed in colorful medical attire inscribing countless words into a her medical journal.

"Excuse me miss, where can I fill this cup with water."

The nurse kept her focus on her journal as she pointed behind her. Aiden raised his eyes and noticed a water jug dispenser against the back wall. He walked around the desk and filled up the glass before he turned around and saw the stacks of paper and files compiled on that nurse's desk. He could only imagine what that work entailed. Especially the kind of work that looked overwhelming.

When he walked back into Sister Gervais room Aiden noticed she had her eyes closed and was breathing heavier than before. Aiden held out the glass in both hands and Sister immediately opened her eyes. Her hands shook as she reached out and her face displayed a look of fatigue. It almost looked as though she was tired and maybe needed a nap.

As she gulped down half the glass of water, Aiden took a seat on the foot of the bed. He knew she probably spent most of the day asleep and didn't want to overwhelm or throw her off balance today. He then internally thought about their conversation earlier, one that made sense. He didn't understand completely what she said but understood the majority of it.

Confusion was a tough feeling to conceal. Aiden reminded himself, these past few weeks, not to let his family or friends witness his confusion. It was a sign of uncertainty, one that would generate many questions and one he didn't have an answer for. What made sense to him lately was the diary. He dreamt many times and at first chance wrote every part of the dream he remembered. He read it over and over and tried to understand what each dream meant. After what Sister Gervais said earlier Aiden knew he had to re-think his viewpoints and what those daydreams really meant. *There had to be a purpose or a reason*. Aiden thought.

Sister Gervais yawned slightly and quickly raised her hand to conceal that yawn.

"Excuse me Aiden."

She then leaned forward with a grin and raised her hand to Aiden.

"How about we take a walk? I'm sure we both could use that exercise to loosen our stiff legs" Sister gave him a delightful grin.

"OK." Aiden said before he reached out and assisted Sister to her feet.

Sister Gervais lightly gripped under Aiden's arm. She was a little shaky but he knew it had to be her seated for such a long time. Once the blood flowed through her veins it would loosen up her joints and muscles. As they slowly stumbled out the door he trailed a step behind Sister adjusting her robe in the back that was raised above her calf muscles.

Sister Gervais led their direction and actually did pick-up speed a bit. Aiden turned his head and viewed her astute posture, one that held a sparkly glow emanating from her face. Her personality was unique but one that he respected.

Near the bathroom she released Aiden and informed him that she will return in a few minutes. He took a seat on a bench beside the bathroom then realized that he wasn't thinking much today just listening. It then dawned on him that no daydreams occurred today as well. He sat up sternly on the bench. This intrigued him. Was it because he was in a spiritual place? Was it because he didn't think much today, or because many minutes have been occupied with conversation? Maybe what Sister Gervais told him earlier was reality.

Aiden had his hands on his knees and shook his head. He knew at home was better than contemplating reality here. That was his judgment and told himself to stick too it.

As Sister left the bathroom and stumbled forward Aiden jumped to his feet and stood beside her as she gripped his arm. She then looked into his eyes.

"Could you proceed with me to the critical care room? There are many friends and Sisters who need support there."

Aiden tapped her hand. "Of course."

As they both staggered down the hallway Aiden noticed a large French glass door that partitioned the end of the hallway. It wasn't a clear view but Aiden could see the medical machines and equipment that occupied the middle of the room and the bed footings were positioned to either side.

Once they reached the doors, Aiden hesitated because he wasn't sure if he should adequately enter such a critical room. Sister Gervais nodded a few times.

"It's alright Aiden. You're with a person who will introduce you to everyone."

Aiden bent his head with a smirk and grabbed the door to slowly pull back. The door was heavy and he felt the weight as he pulled harder. A wind of sorts, one much cooler than the rest of Mont Marie, shot past him from the room. Sister led them through the doorway and into the open area of the room. A few nurse desks were on either sides of the doorway and a nurse occupied one of them.

As Aiden looked around the room he saw another nurse checking vitals on a machine that stood close to a far bed. Sister never stopped taking steps and the both of them got into the center of the open room. There was an open area in the middle, one that was large with medical machines in front and back of them. From the opening he could see all the patients and beds as he turned his head around the room. Not all the beds were filled but the majority was.

Sister Gervais then cleared her throat and placed her hand on Aiden's shoulder. She then swiveled them around to face the glass entrance door.

"Hello Sisters. I want to introduce you to a special boy." Sister's voice was louder and a lot clearer—sounded energetic. "His name is Aiden and is the grandson of Dorothy, a woman who you see in the hallways. She has such a wonderful personality and spirit."

Most of the Sisters opened their eyes or put down their reading materials. A few were weak or asleep because they stayed motionless with closed eyes. A couple of them coughed slowly with a rocky tone that rumbled in their throats. Aiden truly didn't expect or know what to say. He just raised his hand to wave but didn't extend his arm fully.

One of the nurses brought over a chair and slid it behind Sister Gervais. The Sister smiled with a slight head bow as the nurse pressed the chair forward and tapped Sister's shoulder as she sat down. Sister then lightly cleared her throat as the nurse returned with a funny colored book and placed it upon Sister's lap. Aiden automatically thought Sister was going to recite a psalm or scripture as she started to read out words that he was unfamiliar with.

Meanwhile, the nurse dragged over another chair and placed in front of Aiden. She smiled and winked her eye as he sat down. She then placed a cup of water on to a table next to the Sister.

Aiden sat motionless for a few minutes listening to what Sister Gervais was reading. It sounded like either a real life or a fictional wedding story. Some of the critical conditioned Sisters coughed or grinned after some of the sentences Sister recited from the book. She then read an in-depth scene of a bride dressing in attire that was made from silk and the jewels that she wore specifically. It was an in-depth description of a woman getting married and how anxious this woman was.

Aiden then raised his eyebrows and couldn't believe what he was hearing come out of Sister's mouth. She was reading either a real or some fictional story about a wedding.

Aiden held back his head while his mouth dropped open. He pondered this situation for a few seconds because it didn't make a lot sense to him. He always assumed Nuns and Priests lived Holy lives by reading, reciting, and writing religious stuff.

Then reality came too him. His legs shook faster. He felt that certainty finally arisen within him. There were many things he learned every day, some stronger than others, with some good events that were fun or bad events and experiences he just wanted to forget. This was reality and life in its clearest form.

People are people and somewhat the same. Aiden thought faster. It didn't matter if a person was a Nun or a Soldier. People are people. We are just raised with different family, experiences, cultures, and environments. What those people were given or what they chose led them down their future paths in life.

Aiden then halted his thoughts. He quickly wondered if what he now believed was true or not. It certainly was vague and questionable. But too him it made a whole lot more sense.

But all of a sudden he quickly thought about the last wedding he attended. It was his cousin Anne's wedding. Aiden remembered it all only happening a year ago. The wedding ceremony was beautiful within a Cathedral that had an organ raging wondrous music, flowers aligned by walls and pews, plus many friends and the entire family were there. The following reception ceremony flowed perfect with a top of the drawer Disk Jockey, hand made decorations placed throughout the facility, and a cheesy chicken entrée that Aiden loved the most. He then remembered dancing for the first time in public. He was hesitant at first but saw the whole family pound on the dance floor together. The music was groovy enough to shake all their booty's for laughter. Then and only did he experienced the most fun event that night at Anne's wedding reception and that was the Chicken Dance. It was an odd and cheesy dance that everyone laughed at and enjoyed.

Aiden smirked and came back to the present moment where Sister Gervais continued to recite from the book as the nurses performed their treatments. He viewed around the room and noticed that most of the Sisters looked downtrodden and tired. A couple of Sisters had IV injections or other lines attached to them from medical machines. But the majority was just motionless on their beds with unwell looks.

He then gazed over at Sister Gervais. She continued to read but in a much lower tone than before. The area below her eyes looked swelled and her water glass was now empty. He thought highly of her, especially since she read everyday for these terminally ill Sisters.

Aiden stood to his feet and grabbed the Sister's empty glass. Her eyes widened as she looked up and smiled then immediately continued to read. He filled her glass but as he headed back this powerful feeling of sharing overtook his emotions and thoughts. He felt this tingly sensation flow through his nerves and blood. He wasn't quite sure what it was but he knew it involved sharing and helping.

As he put the water glass down Aiden also kneeled in front of Sister Gervais. She continued to read for a few seconds as she looked over the book and directly at him. She then stopped reciting her book and lowered it to her lap.

"Is everything alright Aiden?"

"Yes," He said softly. Then he rose to his feet and smiled. "I like your wedding story Sister but I have a question for you. Have you ever heard of the Chicken Dance?"

Sister's eyes widened as her mouth dropped wide open. "I've heard of it but never have seen it."

Aiden felt his eyebrows shoot higher. "Would you like to see a dance I saw at my cousin Anne's wedding reception?"

Sister Gervais nodded with a grin.

Aiden then looked behind and saw a nurse staring at him.

"Excuse me miss, have you ever heard the Chicken Dance?"

The nurse bobbled her head as she stood to her feet and hurried closer. She aligned herself next to him and blinked with a look of companionship.

Aiden stood tall and raised his arms high. He clinched his fingers together over his thumbs in the shape of a chicken beak. He then nodded to the nurse and harmoniously sang out "Da, na, na, na" as they both flapped their fingers together. The nurse added in and repeated "Da, na, na, na" as they both stuck their hands under their arm pits and swung them up and down like chicken wings. Followed by both swiveling their wastes and legs that got closer to the ground as both kept their upper stature's straight. Then another "Da, na, na, na" sang out as they both swiveled higher and clapped their hands together followed by both jumping to their sides and repeating from the first.

This Chicken Dance continued its theme for a few minutes before both Aiden and the nurse laughed up a storm and caught their breaths. Out of the corner of his eyes Aiden noticed glowing faces that greatly smiled with excitement. The same Sisters who looked dreary and sad now sparkled with happiness. Aiden felt a shiver vibrate through him as his legs started to shake while many in the room clapped.

As Aiden looked over to Sister Gervais, who sparked the most profound and friendliest smile he ever saw, he melted in delight. Her facial expressions for appreciation were evident. Her radiance measured higher than Mount Everest. She then leaned forward and stood quickly before planting the most loving hug around Aiden.

CHAPTER TWENTY-TWO

Katie pondered her serene feelings as Michael drove south on route five. He then made a soft turn and headed up a hill, one that Katie knew well. Her stomach rumbled with anticipation knowing an elegant dinner was at the Log Cabin restaurant. It's been a while since her last visit but Katie loved its comfortable ambience laden with elegantly flavored dishes that were served daily.

The sights surrounding the restaurant entailed spectacular views surrounding the town of Easthampton while the colonial styled interior encompassed a large stone fireplace surrounded by lightly colored walls. For Katie the memories here have been joyous and wonderful being with her friends and family. Tonight was a date that entailed Michael, a friend she always yearned to go deeper with.

After Michael pulled into the entrance way a concierge opened Katie's door. As she stepped out of the car Katie noticed many of the couples were dressier than her and Michael. She mused over this for about half a second before tossing that thought. Michael then stepped out of the car and handed his keys to a valet. Katie stood still and stared upon Michael's eyes.

She would never forget the very first time she met Michael. It was in the break room at work and she had been tired to the point of exhaustion when he stepped in.

There was something about his glowing self-nature that quickly awakened her interest. Their friendship connection was solidified that first day when they talked for an hour that felt like minutes. His down to earth personality immediately lured her interest for him because that was who she is.

They both held hands as they stepped into the Log Cabin foyer. The effervescent smells and ambience made them both smile as maître d' brought them to a window seat. Sunset view was picturesque and focused their vision to the horizon. Katie took all this in as Michael ordered some wine and an escargot appetizer. He knew Katie enough from conversations in the past so when the waiter arrived Michael ordered the prime rib for both. Katie boasted a thankful glance as both of them cheered their glasses together.

"Thank you for today Michael. I'm having a wonderful time."

Michael smiled and took another sip from his wine. Katie has never felt this close to anyone as she had that night. She endured many unfortunate dates. But today was something special for her. She loved being with Michael and knew they were both longing for this get away day.

His eyes portrayed: *thanks so much for openness with you today Katie*. She instantly could see that because her thoughts were the same.

Katie had always wanted to be with someone like that and thought it would always just be a dream. Not today. No dream. Katie leaned forward and grabbed his hands. So warm, so strong, and that enticed her to stare into his eyes.

But then her fingers started to tremble as Aiden entered her thoughts. The first time in many hours that Katie quickly realized she didn't think of her son. A sudden guilt began to overwhelm her. Michael slightly raised his eyebrows with a grin.

"Something has just taken over your thoughts Katie. I can see that." Michael leaned closer. "It's Aiden isn't it?"

Katie raised her head. "Yes."

"He's with Nana so I'm sure he's safe and sound." Michael tapped her hands.

"I know he is. It's just—"

"I completely understand what you're going through and how your son wins your thoughts."

"You're right, I've been emotional lately." Katie smirked. "If I were a tree I would be a Weeping Willow with lots of ants tickling my stem."

Michael sported a large grin and took another sip of wine. "Please feel free to vent with me. I'm a pretty good listener."

"That you are Michael." Katie ran her fingers through her hair. "I apologize for letting these thoughts take over this wonderful dinner. Guess I have some issues that won't go away."

"You're thinking about Aiden's daydreaming aren't you?"

Katie was surprised he knew that. She stared deeply into his eyes.

"It's just that not knowing it all frustrates me. I want the best for Aiden but don't want to get too far into his space. I promised myself to never go that far unless needed."

"That's respectable and direct Katie. Think of it this way, children daydream because of their need to get away from something stressful or unpleasant. They find it easier to retreat to a fantasy world they create for sanctuary. Many psychology books I've read mention that indulging in daydreaming may eventually shut the child out from reality. Now, that's the extreme circumstance and I'm sure you don't view Aiden being that way."

"My son definitely wouldn't let his daydreaming go that far." Katie sat back. "I just wonder what is causing this so that I could take away his confusion and the distance he's been shown lately."

Michael lightly tightened his hands and pulled her closer.

"We are friends and a team. I will be at your beckon call for any help you need?"

Katie blinked her eyes feeling that Michael truly meant what he said. "Thanks."

Both sat back with smiles as the waiter placed their scrumptious dinners on to the table. Katie quickly felt her joyous safe feelings return. She wasn't sure but somehow knew what Michael told her was solid and truthful—he would be there for her. Her comfort and friendship with Michael assured this personal trust.

When Katie got home about eleven, she found only a few lights on in the living room. She walked down the hall and saw Aiden asleep with his head facing away. She quietly closed his door and headed back to the kitchen and filled a cup with water. She then heard a whisper inside the guest bedroom. The door was slightly ajar so Katie lightly knocked and headed in.

Her mother was under her sheets with a dimmed light and a romance novel within her hands.

"Your son is an Angel." Nana said as the largest smile exuded upon her face.

Katie listened to her mother for an hour about the wondrous and dramatic day. This increased Katie's joyous feelings to the point she never experienced before. Her son's events at the medical center meant so much to everyone, but even more to Katie. She emotionally promised her son a big hug in the morning. But even more, she thought about reducing his punishment. *But hold on*, Katie thought to herself, *Aiden's diary means more too him and we have to see if this helps his grades this semester.*

CHAPTER TWENTY-THREE

A blink and then another blink as Aiden mulled over his last day in school for the semester. His testing was completed the day before and today was nothing but a joyous laughter and venting sessions amongst all his classmates. Aiden churned inside not knowing his test grades. He did study but somehow felt he didn't do that well. There were multiple-choice questions on many of his exams and he stuck with C when he wasn't sure. The report card would be the answer and just one he wished never got mailed to his mother.

Everyone in class talked about tests, about summer vacations or activities, and also about next years schedule that teachers handed to students. Pre-Algebra, Integrated Science, Latin, P.E., and Social Studies were the classes for Aiden's first semester. *That's it. I'll start a new beginning and do much better.* Aiden thought to himself as he scrunched his lips and raised his head up and down. He pondered how attentive and focused he would be next semester.

But then a sudden dullness overtook his thoughts. *What happened this year and why did my semesters go downhill in a hurry?* Aiden thought about this for few seconds before he realized he didn't know why. "So confusing. It's so confusing." He said to himself in a soft tone. He then looked out the window and thought about his daydreams. Now that was something he understood and enjoyed.

There were many daydreams in his diary. He read them over, over, and over again. Even the first ones he wrote felt like yesterday. He remembered the details within every daydream; a feeling that made him worthy and worth a damn. These school subjects were in the way and there was no way a homework, a lecture, a test, even a friend would get in his daydream way. Aiden knew this was wrong but it actually made him feel proud.

Suddenly, a class bell rang and the whole class yelped out cheers as they quickly headed for the door. Aiden followed them out and headed to his locker knowing he needed to clean it out and move to a new locker next semester. He turned in his schoolbooks yesterday and that meant all he had in his locker was a few notebooks and school utensils. He placed them in his daypack and closed the door strong.

Aiden took a sigh of relief knowing he was free and clear. He spun back around and saw a light emanate through the glass doors. He felt like personal freedom was through those doors but also knew he didn't talk to many of his friends this past semester. His friends often asked him to do many things. It's just that the diary lured him into more daydreams upon more daydreams. He contemplated the best of this whole situation as he trotted closer to the main door.

It then dawned on him. Aiden halted by the door and watched as Meghan walked solo to the school bus. He was in a minor shock because Meghan always left school with her best friend. Though he barely knew her Aiden felt that he understood who she was. Meghan was one of those girls that held her emotions but showed her expressions like an open window. He didn't know her enough to fully understand her personality but always informed himself that he did know. He revered that every time he saw or thought of her.

She stepped up the stairs as Aiden opened the main door and hurried his pace to the bus. He kept his eyes straight but his peripheral vision was centered on Meghan. She sat in her normal seat, one that was a few rows back but always on the right side. When he reached the door he slowed his speed and trotted up the stairs.

Then a sudden thought quivered his skin and raised his hair on his arms. This sparked feeling began to overtake his emotions and steer his vision into blurriness. Aiden then stopped and took a deep breath because he knew a daydream was on its way. "This is not a good time." He said quietly to himself. He reached over and pinched his arm hard. "Ouch!" He twisted instead of pinched and that truly hurt more than he thought.

The bus driver chewed his gum and displayed a funny stare directly at Aiden. This driver has always been strange and empowered himself as commander whenever he sat in his captain's chair. Aiden tried to ignore his looks and grunts whenever the driver disliked something because he always sounded annoyed. But this moment was different, the driver focused on him and that meant he was the new irritation.

Aiden shook his head and continued up the stairs. He saw Meghan staring out the window and felt a sudden comfort knowing she didn't see what just happened. He then sucked his stomach in tight because he was going to sit parallel to her. This was first for him. Aiden didn't know what was empowering him to be so brave. He always thought of Meghan but never had the guts to talk with her about anything.

As he sat on the seat, Aiden placed his bag next to himself then looked forward whistling kindly. He tapped his legs gently then sped up with power and speed. He then slapped his hands and spun himself to the side as his legs caught-up to his upper torso a second later. He raised his head and looked directly into her eyes.

"Hi Meghan."

She quickly spun her head over and threw a grin. "Hello Aiden." She then quickly looked away. Aiden sucked in a lot of air.

"Isn't it great that it's summer? Do you have any vacations or big plans for the next few months?" Aiden abruptly stopped and instantly thought of himself as being annoying. He chuckled for a second and started to feel his veins pound as his heart raced faster. Meghan looked back into his eyes.

"No big plans that I know of. My father and I normally vacation for a week in Newburyport with family."

"Newburyport is nice." Aiden instantly thought of all his experiences there. "I'm sure you go to Salisbury Beach or Plum Island, go on Whale Tours, and see all the sites in the area. There's a lot to do there. It's wicked fun."

Meghan expressed an impressed look. "So you've been there?"

"We normally go to York Beach in Maine and camp in a trailer close to the beach and we have vacationed on Plum Island when I was much younger. We stayed at my aunt's friend's house close to the beach. I remember walking for hours in the bird sanctuary and collecting sand dollars all the time. My cousins and I would count them and the one with the most always won. We also one night, during that week, went to Salisbury beach and played all the arcade games and ride the fun rides, like the bumper cars and water car rides."

Aiden then stopped himself. He noticed Meghan's eyes grow larger the more he talked. She cleared her throat.

"Wow! You definitely have been to many places in the summer. Your family sure takes care of you." Meghan mentioned in a sarcastic tone but with a facial expression of interest.

"Yeah, my family is close. We always go on vacations together. I guess it helps pay for things and all of us stick together for fun." Aiden then thought of Meghan. "Do you go to Newburyport with your family?"

"My family is my father and my uncle who lives in Springfield. My grandparents passed away a few years ago and my uncle is not doing so well."

Aiden frowned. "Sorry to hear that. How about your mother?"

Meghan sat still for a few seconds as her eye blinking increased. "My mother lives in Daytona, Florida."

A burst of curiosity excited Aiden. He instantly thought about Meghan's similarities with him. He then jetted back to his daydream of Daytona 500. He grew a large smile the same time Meghan's face formed a curious look.

"So you've been to Florida?"

"No. I just dream of one day going to the Daytona 500."

"Oh." She said, keeping her voice level low.

"When's the last time you visited your mother?"

Meghan's eyes vanished from the conversation, returning a second later with saddened looks. "I can't remember the last time I saw my mother."

She then silenced herself, crossed her arms, and stared forward. Many kids started entering the bus and chatting-up a storm. This was the last day of school and many were excited to go home for a few months.

Aiden recognized the glared facial expression that Meghan displayed. He knew it well because his father barely visited and hardly spent time with him. Aiden then reacted on instinct; he knew Meghan had drifted off into unfortunately bad thoughts. Aiden liked this because there was another person similar to him. He wasn't a loner when it came to living with a single parent and fighting to get back a family. The look in Meghan's eyes obviously meant the same for her.

The bus ride home was quicker than normal as Aiden thought of his conversation with Meghan. He loved the fact that he somehow got the power to talk with her and especially liked how much they actually had in common when it came to family. When the school bus driver abruptly stopped and swung the creaky door open Meghan stepped to her feet and smiled at Aiden as she headed off. He gasped as she walked down the road.

CHAPTER TWENTY-FOUR

A sudden announcement loudly rang as Katie stopped typing due to her shaky hands. Those internal broadcasts hurt her ears. Many workers often complained about those noisy disturbances with no fix. Go figure. A pile of data sheets was the norm for her office but this pile was ridiculous being stacked far above her inbox.

Katie looked over and, of course, Julie was sitting back and laughing on the phone. *That woman sure knows how to relax.* Katie contemplated as she grabbed the next data sheet. She then sat back and scratched her eyes. This itchiness equaled her soreness when it came to staring into a computer screen all day.

Suddenly, the door opened quickly and this hunk of a man strode into the room. Michael had a smile the size of Texas as he got closer. He stood tall, kept silent, and tapped his sides when he reached the desk. Katie knew some big news was concealed but hopefully some good news at least. She beamed a blink his way as he looked through the glass windows and flung around to plant a soft kiss. What a kiss that was! Katie perched herself tall in her seat with a reenergized feeling. Michael sat at the edge of her desk.

"I got some good news for you." Michael raised his eyebrows. "Mr. Sordun mentioned in our meeting today about invitations for the company's summer picnic being sent today."

Katie flared her nostrils. She knew that meant the men would be having fun at the picnic because the women employees were never invited. Even the male employee's families were never invited. It surely was a booze festival for sure but that's what the ladies always knew. Michael kept his head erect and looked over to Julie.

"Listen ladies."

Julie told her friend that she would call back and hung up the phone.

Michael stood and looked both ways. "This year's summer picnic will be for every employee and be located at High Meadows in Granby, Connecticut. The picnic will be in two weeks with no worries because it's being catered and there will be many mobile attractions set-up like a trampoline, sporting equipment for the kids, a large pool, and many more game events."

Katie noticed Julie's strange look but then again she was shocked herself. This male chauvinist company has always held male events. She assumed it was whatever happens at their party's stays at their parties. At least that's what the gossipy ladies passed to each other.

Julie got up from her seat and headed for the door. "Thanks Michael." She said loudly as she hurried down the hallway.

Katie giggled a bit. "That invitation gossip will spread faster than the mailroom can send it out."

Michael bobbed his head as he watched Julie move faster than a cheetah. "That's what I'm guessing."

He then looked back and bowed his head. "I know you've been the lead feminist for this company and I salute you for that. This male dominated company has done nothing to this point to bring you ladies the respect you all deserve. You all work just as hard as most of the males in here. I honestly believe that Mr. Sordun respects you because he always listened to your comments about fairness. I've even heard him re-state what you mentioned to him in meetings."

Meghan felt her forehead wrinkle as Michael spoke. He then pulled a chair closer.

"Mr. Sordun has actually met with all the supervisors and managers to discuss women in the workplace and equality when it came to viewing their work performance. He showed them charts on how production from women is surpassing most men in the company. He's basically attempting to change their mindsets. So, let's see how this goes. I do believe it will work because Mr. Sordun would have to answer to you." Michael pointed his finger.

Katie truly didn't know what to say. There was a bunch of excitement that equaled many questions. A bunch of truisms that Katie knew would take time to display reality. Michael was the most honest man in this company and she trusted him. At least that's what Katie believed but she always took one step at a time in regards to everything. She definitely learned that from her past dating experiences.

She and Michael had a few more dates since the first due to their busy lives. One of the dates, Katie viewed it as one, was a luncheon close to work. It didn't matter when or where they dated because Katie yearned for their time together to learn more about each other. The first date was comfortable but the rest were even more comfortable. They both opened to each other about who they were and how they view the world around them. So much in common, so many down to earth similarities, and that exuded comfy feelings. How could anything be better than that? Katie never experienced such a relationship but it still sparked many questions because she believed nothing was perfect. She then clinched her eyebrows.

"The company picnic sounds like fun. I can only guess the company will change over the years and transfer to a good ole person's network instead of boys. I've told you before and don't want to sound like a skipping record but this male dominated management always hurts the women employees. It's extremely evident and all of us ladies instantly see that. Granted, we are happy to have a job, it pays the bills, and our society is changing faster than this company recognizes. The women in the corporate world are not there yet as many other companies are changing faster than this one."

Katie let out a deep breath and overtly shook her lips.

"OK, enough of that blah, blah, stuff. Do you plan on taking Meghan to the picnic?"

Michael tossed a blink her way. "I sure do. Meghan's done a great job with school this year by increasing her grades in the subject areas that hurt her last year. She deserves rewards, even little ones we call picnics. It sure gets us out of the house. The more time I spend with my daughter is my reward. I see this picnic rewarding the both of us. How about you?"

Katie hesitated with a response because her thoughts drifted. She instantly thought how Aiden's school year was an exact opposite to what Michael mentioned about his daughter's school year. His grades got shoddier every semester while Meghan's grades rose. *What does that mean*? Katie's view swirled in circles. She then focused back to Michael.

"I sure am taking the little pumpkin. He will have a great time playing the games."

Michael nodded. "That's great." He then stood to his feet. "Oh yeah. Are you still OK with a dinner Friday night?"

Katie internally trembled. She forgot about that date invitation yesterday and didn't ask her mother last night about it. But that didn't matter, she assumed, because her mother never minded sleeping in her daughter's homes. She crossed her fingers under her desk.

"A date it is." Katie formed a grin.

Michael's prominent stature headed towards the door. Katie lost thoughts for a second viewing his behind swaying back and forth. A mini sensual observation made her moment even more joyous.

She then shook her head thinking she was making too much of that. Their relationship was still in its birthing stages and forming it's future with every contact they made. She lusted Michael in more ways than one and made it certain that she wouldn't show or tell him about any of that until they reached that point. *Where and when is that point?* Katie thought as she lightly giggled. A friendship starting point had already passed and now the further matters were bound to increase. Those matters were uncertain as Katie knew it best to let them ride.

But what am I going to wear Friday night? Katie thought as she felt a churning sensation in her stomach, something akin to anxiety.

"Oh, I'm not thinking about this further it's going to emotionally poop me out." She voiced out loud and then looked around the empty room.

A sudden avalanche of guilt overwhelmed her noggin. She told a little fib. It wasn't a lie, it just wasn't the truth, or maybe not the solid truth, its just how she felt. She looked up at the clock and saw that she had another half hour till her day ended.

"As soon as I get home I'm calling my mother." Katie gently said to herself.

Chapter Twenty-Five

Waves crashed loudly on to the beach as Aiden squashed his toes into the white sand taking joyous steps. The sky was perfectly clear displaying a dark blue ambience that warmed his surroundings with sun rays flowing from above. A flock of seagulls chirped louder the closer they flew along the shore.

Meghan's walked pleasantly as Aiden picked-up his pace. The bird sanctuary sign was just ahead. They both sought after the rolling sand dunes that were so close, so near, and within visual proximity. He turned his torso and jogged sideways crossing his legs over and over again. Meghan's face illuminated a joyous smile as she kept up the tempo. Her one-piece bathing suit was elegantly colored to match her astonishing blue eyes.

As they caught up to the sand dunes laden with beach grass Meghan brought him into an alcove. The surroundings looked so prehistoric which made them feel surreal and inviting. Meghan flopped gracefully to the sand and lured Aiden down by elegantly curling her index finger. That invitation sent shivers though his system—ones he never felt before. He fell to his knees feeling the soft and light sand rebound. The salty wind whipped through his hair as he lay beside her soft side.

He then looked into the sky and noticed a solitary puffed cloud slowly passing by. The wind speed suddenly increased spurring many sand pebbles that flowed past them. The cloud then changed shape in the form of a racing horse. It's legs gallantly flexed and moved at a racing speed. Aiden flexed his hand and pointed upward toward the cloud. He heard Meghan voice an amazed sound as they both locked eyes together and smiled.

There was a feeling that powered sensation and drew Aiden closer to Meghan. He closed his eyes and perched his lips. A kiss was planted upon his forehead. His heart pitter-pattered in delight but he also questioned why his forehead? She wrapped her arms around his shoulders and began to stroke the back of his head.

"Good evening honey." Meghan's lips moved but her stern voice sounded similar to mom.

Aiden hesitated for a second and shook his head . . .

The kitchen light turned on brightly as Aiden saw his mother place her purse down on to the counter. She was home and he didn't hear her enter the front door. Aiden looked up at the clock and noticed it was 4:10 in the afternoon. He then shot his glance back to mom who filled the coffee maker with water. He thought of how deep he must have been in his daydream. *How could I not hear her open the door?* A second later he started to feel lost even though he was sitting at his dinning room table where he initially sat.

Mom filled the coffee pot with water and scooped grounded beans into the filter before she pressed the ON button. Aiden then thought back to the daydream and how real it seemed. He could smell a bit of java but his scents still resided at the beach with the salty smell and the sand between his toes. So real that daydream felt. He then thought of his mother's voice and if it was either she or Meghan he kissed. *It was Meghan*! Just the thought of mom being the one he kissed made Aiden feel ill for a second then he quietly chuckled.

He opened his diary notebook and started to write down the start to finish contents of his daydream. Away he went into diary land.

A sudden and surreal yawn was then heard. It was strange due to its longevity and strange tone. This made Aiden slip back effortlessly to prior years when his mother displayed many differing sounds that exuded a character change. Yes, but more, it was an emotional change. Aiden hesitated and stopped scribbling into his diary. This meant more than normal, it meant something was changing within his mother and that sparked intrigue, plus many uncertain questions.

That was just it, uncertainty. There were many occasions that he remembered his mother's emotions shuffling to the extremes. Most were exuberant and giggly to the point of Aiden's sensations following suit. There were ghastly emotions, one's that infected everyone she came into contact with. Aiden hid deep within his personal caves to exude that contempt. The bizarre piece to this was that his behavior brought his mother back to normal quicker than anything or anyone else. This certainly perplexed Aiden and somewhat made him happy knowing he might have sparked a happier change.

Was that true or not? That was his question and one he considered himself too young to figure out. Then a light went off in his noggin—a light of wonderment. Could this truly be himself initiating her mood swings that threw away interest and enticed guilt? He was her only child and that meant a bunch of attention and responsibility and also love and interest. Aiden knew he did a good job because he heard his mother preach to him about how much she respected and loved him.

Mom then picked up the phone and started dialing. She leaned back against the counter as she smiled and began talking. Aiden instantly knew it was Nana because mom always used a devoted and down to earth verbal tone. She talked about the day and then asked Nana if she was OK sleeping over the house Friday night. That definitely threw the interest flag up high as Aiden wondered what was going to happen. It then dawned on him that she was dating Michael from work and that man was acceptable, more than any other, because he got along with him every time they met. Michael was a nice guy and one Aiden always enjoyed chatting with. He just never knew his last name and never asked his mother. He figured it didn't matter or maybe was too much information. The last thing he wanted to do was cross some personal path too fast.

As she hung up the phone mom filled her coffee cup then stirred in milk and sugar droppings. She then winked as she sat across the table. Normally her tiredness exuded upon her face and Aiden was used to that. That exuberant look drew him into wanting more information.

"Mom, you look so happy today and I heard you mention to Nana about Friday night. You have a date with Michael?"

Mom swallowed her sip of coffee and sat back in her chair. "I sure do have a date with Michael. He's taking me to some restaurant. He never mentioned which one and I didn't ask."

Aiden bobbed his head with a grin. "You like that intrigue mom, it fascinates you not knowing which place or food you will have. I always think of 007 and James Bond movies when that happens. It's like a spy trick or unknown event that charms you."

Mom displayed a look of amazement. "I'm impressed with the way you mentioned that." She sat silent for a second or two and then smiled. "You sure do make me proud to be you mother with all your different analogies you provide me."

Aiden felt his eyebrows drop in curiosity. "Analogies? I don't even know what that means."

She giggled and took another sip of coffee. "You compare my delighted desires perfectly. You certainly amaze me my son and do it very well. We are best friends and that keeps us going in life very well." Mom shot a grin. "Yes, very well."

It then dawned on Aiden, a question he meant to ask his mother for days. "I forgot to ask you Mom about our summer vacation. Are we going to York Beach or Plum Island this year?"

Katie paused. "Good question." She took another sip of coffee. "I apologize for not thinking about our vacation yet. It's just that this year has been so busy with all this work and other matters." She then shot her eyebrows higher. "I will ask your godparents, Pete and Shirley, this weekend and see if we can spend a week in their trailer at Camp Eaton. Maybe we can go in July or early August."

Aiden thought back to all the vacations he took at York Beach, the campfires at night, the Long Sands beach walks in the mornings, feasting on saltwater taffy all day, and visiting the York's Wild Kingdom and Amusement Park. All these events were fun and relaxing even though he felt tired on the ride home. It's like he needed a vacation from his vacation.

Excitement started to flow through his veins. He knew the vacation wasn't reticent at this point but a vacation to the beach was the world. Fun was abound to happen in the near future and that meant making some kind of plans.

CHAPTER TWENTY-SIX

Katie awakened with curiosity Saturday morning. The sunlight glared through the blinds as she stretched herself into a thought. A lot of paraphernalia and hype about the summer picnic excited all the company's employees, especially the women. Today was the day Mr. Sordun forecasted to be the joyous start to the company's coed yearly events; huge promises for sure but definitely a starting point for increased equality and happiness throughout the company. Katie had her fingers crossed.

As she strutted down the hallway and conducted her morning activities Katie halfheartedly felt her desires and anticipation for today. There were many inside questions she asked herself with no literal answers because she just didn't know how today would really be or how Mr. Sordun coordinated the picnic. She then fluffed off her anticipation and worries because today was a full day with Aiden.

The car trunk was filled with cases of soda due to individual employees acquiring items to fill this picnic puzzle with side items or party pieces. It was a catered picnic but Mr. Sordun still asked employees to bring a specific side item before he gave them a check to pay for it. His rationale for this was teamwork and that rolled many eyes within the company.

Katie made sure she filled her gas tank yesterday, just in case the weight of the soda, or a sudden traffic jam, or the driving distance being too far. She always worst-case planned every trip and event. It only took one maybe two set backs to figure that out. This day wouldn't have any of that.

Katie wasn't a perfectionist. She clearly knew that and an experiential learner was her main stay and belief in life. Why experience the same problem twice—that was credence—because that would make her feel naughty and dim-witted not to mention ignorant. There would be none of that.

Aiden was half-asleep as he stumbled out the door with the bag of extras that Katie asked him to bring. That bag was filled with her extreme necessities like umbrella, raincoat, water, flashlight, and another pair of socks just in case. Aiden always grunted packing those items until he learned to keep a side bag filled with those articles in his closet. What a smart kid, Katie thought, and then again he was the focus to her life.

Katie locked her front door and hesitated for a few seconds. Her recent spotlight has been transformed into thinking about two men. Michael was starting to empower her emotions and thoughts. *By no reason does that mean anything less for Aiden.* Katie stumbled through her thoughts quickly. A sudden ambush of guilt sparked some kind of overwhelming shiver and blood flow increase.

As Aiden yawned and closed the trunk of the car Katie smiled feeling his presence overtaking her guilt. This surly attitude was going to stop now. The last thing Katie needed was emotional diatribe to overwhelm her trip to the picnic. She jumped into the driver's seat and stroked the back of Aiden's neck as he yawned with his mouth ever so extended.

"Someone looks tired. Did you get any sleep last night?" Katie casually said.

Aiden slowly swished his head form side-to-side. "I read through my diary last night and when I looked at the clock noticed it was three in the morning." He then lay back against the headrest. "I couldn't believe it because I started reading around nine o'clock last night."

Katie smiled. "You are such a dedicated boy when it comes to your punishment."

Aiden shot an anguished look as he raised an eyebrow. "Yeah, I sure am punished because you have me addicted to this diary." He then grinned. "I've actually lost count to how many daydreams I've had and annotated within this diary."

"Annotated?" Katie blinked as Aiden perched a quick stare into her eyes. "I'm impressed with the sophisticated wording you use." She then lightly giggled.

Aiden shot an attentive facial look. "Those dictionary and synonym books you gave me are great. I use them constantly to describe items I don't know how to spell or what they mean."

"I'm impressed with you my son. Looks as though English will be your next best graded class."

Aiden blinked slowly. "I didn't think of that."

"How many pages have you written?"

He opened his notebook and tossed through the pages. "Good question. I've noticed that I'm pretty close to filling this whole notebook."

Katie gazed over as she started the car. She noticed the front and back of all the pages were crammed full of wording and sketches. "I'm impressed because that notebook has several hundred pages."

As she put the shift into drive Katie handed Aiden the map and directions.

"OK honey, you are the navigator. Please make sure we're headed in the right direction.

Aiden spun the map around and looked curiously at the routes. He read through the directions quickly and threw his thumb up high with an austere face. "I'm the navigator and will guide us there pilot . . . I mean miss . . . or Mom." Aiden pointed to the left on Canal Street as Katie reached the end of the driveway. "Take a left."

Katie shook her head with a giggle as she turned and slapped his knee lightly.

Chapter Twenty-Seven

Aiden spoke diligently giving his mother directions to the picnic. Suddenly, a large High Meadow's sign, one that pointed an arrow for direction, caught his attention. He tapped Mom's shoulder.

"Take the next left."

Mom winked. "Will do honey."

As they pulled into the half-filled parking lot a guy wearing a red vest directed them down a parking lane behind the other vehicles. Further down the way another member blew his whistle and pointed them into a parking spot. Mom pulled in, turned the car off, and opened the trunk by pulling the handle under the steering wheel.

Aiden simultaneously walked to the rear of the car and noticed that Mom had her lips perched together displaying an amazed look as a staff worker rolled a large flat-bedded cart close to the trunk.

"Good morning. I'm here to assist you in transporting your items into the park. Miss, are you here for the company picnic?"

Mom hesitated for a second. "Yes, we are here for the picnic."

The worker smiled and began lifting the soda packs out of the trunk and arranging them perfectly on to the cart. Aiden stood there impressed. He leaned in a few times to help the worker but knew he would be in his way. The worker amazed them both as he finished stacking the soda packs with ease and quickness.

"Miss, I just need your name to pass to the picnic's director."

"Katie Ellis."

The worker wrote diligently on his notepad. "Thank you Ms. Ellis." He pointed his finger. "Just follow the path to the main pavilions. They will be to the left of the pony ring." He then pushed the cart forward with utter ease.

A sudden thin cloud passed over Aiden—a smoky wood grill odor drew him to a forward stroll in its direction. Mom followed suit. In the near distance were a bunch of kids playing games along the fields. To his immediate left Aiden was astonished seeing the sand volleyball court in the distance and several horseshoe pits closer. Just beyond those were shuffleboard and badminton courts followed by a large and perfectly conditioned baseball diamond.

Aiden felt his heart rate increase as excitement shot through his veins. Then he halted feeling his Mom bump into him as she gathered her tickets out of her purse. There was a large white tent that was structured to the side of the large wooden pavilion and just beyond was the largest pool Aiden ever saw. The deep blue water sparkled as the sun shined brighter and brighter. His mouth dropped wide open as Mom tapped his shoulder.

"This park is amazing, isn't it honey?"

"Ah huh!" Aiden drooled as he swiped his hand over his mouth.

Further down the path Aiden started seeing Mom's co-workers and a sign that pointed into a large wooden pavilion door. She exchanged greetings as they both headed in and saw the internal decorations that inspired both their excitements. Several large wooden foundation poles sprung into the high ceilings and were spread down a long row laden with white table covers.

All the buffet tables were gathered along the wall and had heated dishes flowing as far as the eye could see. In between the tables was an oval shaped bar railing, one that exuded a cedar stained sparkle. Within the bar itself was a tremendously large black metal stove that ran a chimney through the roof—two men with large white chef hats opened the metal doors showing large orange colored flames that bellowed graciously inside. Further down was a table that held numerous chillers and that's where the worker stopped his cart and began unpacking the soda.

Aiden was amazed. He never saw such a large indoor pavilion and especially one that had walls strewn with artistic campground paintings and pictures. He shook his head thinking he was making too much of it. His anticipation about today's events excited him greater.

Introductions were provided to Aiden as his mother met with her co-workers—she hugged the majority of them. The conversations turned to the women displaying amazement about how such a picnic thrilled them greater than all expected. Just being there meant more to them than anything else.

Aiden took a few steps back and felt a hand touch his head and shake his hair. He twisted around and saw Michael with a large grin.

"Hi there Aiden. I'm glad you and your mother made it and I hope you both have a great time. There are so many things for you to do here." Michael spoke faster than he normally did. A sparkle of joy exuded from his face.

He then stepped to the side and opened his arms for Mom as she moved closer and nestled into his tight hug. The joyous stare she planted in Michael's eyes was more than Aiden's ever seen and that enticed him to view more and more. Moms glowing facial happiness landed a pulse that was thudding in Aiden's ears. He internally was experiencing a feeling never felt before. It was funny and strange and meant the world to see his mother being so happy with another person. This was a telltale sign that Mom was in love.

Michael looked back at Aiden. "Let's go out to the deck area. It's beautiful out there and I promise you both will like it. Besides, I reserved a table for all of us."

Aiden trailed a step behind, taking in all the sights, as they walked through large wooden French style doors. The majority of the crowd was already on the large deck as they entered the area with many folks occupying all the tables and were chatting up a storm. To the right was a large and circular bar that had every seat filled to the brim.

As they dodged people between the tables Aiden thought he noticed someone special. He clinched his eyebrows in anticipation trying to view the person but the crowd was constantly scuttling in front of them. Then all of a sudden, there it was, an opening of the crowd as they approached closer.

Aiden then felt his jaw drop in utter amazement. He kept stepping forward without even perceiving who it was. Meghan! Her hair fell into waves around her glossy face as she stared off into the pool. She faced sideways keeping her stature erect and alert. Several folks walked by motioning to her about the table and she put her hand down and shook her head as taken.

A sudden numbness flowed through his body and Aiden didn't know what to think. His wits spiked and swerved around in circles, as he got closer.

Once they reached the table Meghan stood tall shaking Mom's hand as Michael introduced her. Then he looked back and stuck his open hand out nonchalantly asking Aiden to come closer. It was time. This was it.

Meghan's lips curved up into a ready smile. Her comforted facial expression meant she knew about this connection. Aiden's fingers were trembling as he opened his hand and reached forward. A few more steps and he slightly stumbled flexing an embarrassing looking chin. He knew this greeting meant more than he could understand. That was everything too him, at least for the moment.

Aiden followed suit as Mom and Michael sat into their chairs. Michael sat next to Meghan and continued his glance into Aiden's eyes.

"This is my daughter Meghan." He then swerved his stare and blinked at his daughter. "Meghan, this is Katie the woman I've been telling you so much about, and her son, Aiden."

Meghan elegantly bowed her head while still glimpsing at Mom. "It's a pleasure to meet the woman my father has been continually saying good things about." She then reached her hand out and tapped Aiden's arm. "It's also good to see you again. How is your summer going?"

Aiden then realized his mouth was wide open. He jetted his hand up to scoop away any moisture. Simultaneously mom reached her hand out and shook Meghan's.

"It's wonderful to finally meet you Meghan. Your father talks about you all the time." She then leaned closer with a quieter voice. "No worries your father doesn't tell me anything personal about you, he just tells me how swollen with pride he is for you and also how deeply he loves you."

The three of them sparked a joyous conversation and altogether started to giggle. Aiden sat back stunned and never took his eyes off Meghan. He still didn't know what to think. He felt anguished in so many ways he just couldn't explain. He never put two and two together and a feeling of stupidity overwhelmed him greater than he perceived anything. But he knew etiquette, his mother taught him well, and he stayed quiet. Even though his tongue swelled in grief Aiden shot a grin and nodded his head as he looked over to Michael who winked.

"The buffet begins in an hour. However, drinks are ready for all of us." He then looked towards Meghan and Aiden. "Are both of you good with sweet tea?"

Meghan slightly raised her eyebrows and nodded. He then looked into Aiden's eyes before blinking a yes. He swerved his look towards mom.

"How about you join me as we get some tasty beverages?"

Mom raised her shoulders. "OK."

They both stood tall and headed towards the bar. Aiden watched them get further but heard Meghan let out a sudden sigh. He quickly glanced over and saw her glancing down to his hand, one that was tapping his diary.

"What's that you have under your hand?"

"Oh this?" Aiden's voice was not as steady as he wanted it to be. He cleared his throat "It's just a notebook I write on." He said halfheartedly before he realized he was fibbing. Meghan widened her eyes.

"What kind of notes?"

Aiden swallowed feeling too emotional and guilty to speak. All he did was nod his head for a few seconds. He didn't know what to say but spoke in his sternest voice. "Just notes about what I've experienced in life."

Meghan sat motionless for a second then giggled. "I hope you don't write about me after today."

He opened his mouth to say something but the truth died on his lips. "I won't write anything about you."

Then her nose turned in a sneered fashion. "So I'm not an experience in your life?"

Aiden then mumbled with no wording.

Meghan let out a deafening laugh. "I'm just kidding Aiden." She then pointed over to the field. "Wanna play some badminton?"

"Sure!"

Meghan stood tall and headed towards the stairs. She flowed heedlessly with every step as Aiden followed directly behind her hoping she would teach him how to play this sport he never participated in.

CHAPTER TWENTY-EIGHT

With their hands filled with drinks Katie and Michael strode back to the table. They both noticed the kids heading toward the field and their mirrored strides enlightened their thoughts. Katie made sure to count their bags sitting along the table. She innately was a worrywart and that made her feel more secure accounting for personal items.

Once they placed the drinks down and wiggled their hands free Katie noticed that Aiden left his diary on the table. That was bizarre, Katie thought, looking at the roughed-up notepad. He never left the diary anywhere because it was a permanent fixture to his sides for weeks.

Michael opened his arms for Katie and she moved closer nestling into his tender embrace. He hugged tighter then swiveled his head closer and planted a large kiss on her cheek.

"It's so good to see you. How was your ride today?"

"Quicker than we expected. Aiden did a great job navigating us here." Katie then faced him. "That boy is growing quicker than I ever imagined."

Michael bobbed his head. "He sure is." He stuck his hands out with a grin. "You will blink one day and realize your son is graduating high school. Time sure flies being our age."

Michael then grabbed her hands.

"The first time I was introduced he was knee high to a grasshopper and so quiet. I threw some jokes his way before he opened up enough to speak his mind. I don't blame him a bit because I was the same way growing up and completely understand his viewpoint."

Katie steadily gazed into his eyes. "His personality is still building and I only hope I can make his growing path clear ahead. That boy makes me so proud the way he's budding into adulthood."

Michael raised his eyebrow. "Adulthood? That boy has many fun years ahead to learn and experience life's joys. I consider childhood as freedom to do and think all that's new. It's just the way to learn what life's all about. He will get to adulthood faster than you think he will and I recommend you let him soar to the heights through childhood."

Katie reached down and pulled the diary closer. "He sure is expressing his life into this notebook." She then took a seat followed by Michael. "He's been having these daydreams that take over his attention in class and home." She then twiddled her fingers on the diary. "I just wish I knew what was causing him to vision away his time further into daydreaming and not school work. He says that he does try to pay attention in his classes but his thoughts drift away from what is being taught."

Michael's lips moved back and forth like a saw. "That is interesting to say the least. Obviously something is bothering him and he doesn't know how to deal with it or maybe he doesn't even know what it is. Most boys will anguish themselves by either fighting or displaying rebelliousness to any tasking put upon them. It's hard to explain the nature behind those rowdy moods. I was told growing up that my behavior was because I didn't care. My parents punished me into more hate. You're obviously not taking that wrong path. You're doing the right thing and letting him vent his frustrations and feelings on paper."

Katie smiled. "You and I think alike. The last thing I wanted to happen was taking away anything from him because I thought that would backfire both of us in many ways. I figured that providing him a tool, the diary, to write down his worries would be a way for him to feel better. I did express to him that the diary was a punishment for his poor grades."

"He obviously isn't seeing it as a punishment especially since he's spending so much time writing all those thoughts down on to paper."

Katie agreed by blinking faster; she was still awe struck about how similar Michael's viewpoints were to her very own. He then questioned her with a grin.

"Have you read any portions of his diary to see what his frustrations are?"

Katie raised her eyebrow. "You are kidding me." She said lightheartedly. "Aiden keeps that diary close to him wherever he goes. He even sleeps with it in his bed. Life and work have just been a little overwhelming lately and the last thing I would want to do is nurture Aiden into explaining himself. He will talk too me when he wants to talk too me."

"Sounds like you have a plan and are sticking to it."

"That is the plan." She then tapped the diary more. "But I must admit this is the first I've seen the diary away from him."

"He's having fun with Meghan." Kevin glanced over to the field. "Look at them swing those badminton paddles. Boy o boy I sure do remember playing that sport when I was their age."

Katie nodded with a wink then heard a deeply toned laugh—one she pinpointed. She spun her head and noticed Mr. Sordun shaking lots of hands as he weaved his way closer. His Hawaiian shirt looked stylish as it flowed over his linen styled pants. In addition, he let his facial hair grow and made Katie believe he was an actor from Magnum P.I. or Hawaii Five-O. He did look more like Tom Selleck so it had to be Magnum P.I.

As he passed by the last few tables Mr. Sordun headed directly for them and flaunted a shiny smile. He was an artistic type and always expressed to Katie about the theater show he took his wife to or what book he read the night before. He sure did tell her almost everyday about how he found her the most comfortable to talk to.

"Hello Katie and Michael. Hope your enjoying those drinks?"

Katie winked. "Aloha, Mr. Magnum P.I."

Mr. Sordun smirked as he dove into a character role. "Aloha! My red Ferrari is just around the corner." He replied stroking of his mustache.

"You're going to have to show us your mobile man jewels Mr. Magnum." Michael then snorted.

All three of them broke down into hilarious sounds. Each of the laughing spurts echoed significantly followed by teary eyes in Katie's view. Seeing Mr. Sordun leak a bit of his margarita on to his pants topped it all. He sat down into the chair and started wiping his pants with his napkin.

Michael began sparking a conversation as Katie took in all the humor. Mr. Sordun always amazed her. He was quite the professional with his stature but action wise he displayed comfort. That was who he was and Katie respected him.

She then glanced over to the field watching Aiden and Meghan as they swung their tiny rackets and flung a little plastic birdie over the net. This picnic was sure comforting. Through her periphery sights Katie noticed Michael also looking down the field. They watched their little ones having a great time for a few minutes. Simultaneously, they both shot looks at each other and smiled in joy.

But then, Katie's smile drooped to a straight face noticing Mr. Sordun reading through Aiden's diary. *He was silent and she didn't notice him leave the table in the last few minutes.* Katie thought quickly before her emotions started to ache. She just assumed the diary was forbidden and that was her internal mantra and no others.

Nervousness jolted through her body as she noticed Michael look directly at her with his mouth dropped wide open. Her breathing started to become uneven as she looked around and noticed the party patrons having a blast of a time as they all sat back and enjoyed each other. Katie jetted her vision back and saw Mr. Sordun look so tranquil, yet so vehemently focused, to every page within the diary as he turned each page faster and faster.

He then darted a glance, one laden with intrigue.

"If you don't mind me asking Katie, who's is this?"

Katie took a deep breath. "It's my son's notebook."

"I only read a few pages but was drawn in to read more and more. Aiden's literature style is incredible, especially the way he describes scenes with astonishing wording and viewpoints." He took another sip of his margarita. "Your son is either gifted or you sure taught him how to write like a talented author."

"Ah . . ." Katie opened her mouth and no words came out. She began to feel tears dribble over her cheeks.

Michael tapped her arm. "It's OK Katie." He then looked at Mr. Sordun. "That's actually a diary of Aiden's daydreams, one's that have overwhelmed his life lately. That diary is Katie's form of punishment for his bad grades in school and it seems to be the best way for him to let out his frustrations and re-coup. Katie hopes this diary will increase his attention in school with better grades next semester."

"That's an exquisite way of explaining that Michael." Mr. Sordun gently tapped Katie's shoulder. "I never would of thought about such a punishment. I commend you Katie. Both my kids are in college and my son is a radical who rebelled against every thing I asked him to do. He did things by himself and I kept my fingers crossed that he wouldn't fail or get hurt." Mr. Sordun lifted his head, kissed his hand, and raised it high. "I'm blessed to have him in college and he sure is gaining his manhood and professionalism very well."

Katie swallowed hard. "That's wonderful Mr. Sordun. I guess some kids require distance from their parents and your son is talented with a good head on his shoulders."

"Thanks Katie." He then ran his fingers over his mustache. "What happened to me being Magnum P.I.?"

Katie and Michael's lips curved into a ready smile. Mr. Sordun then fluttered through more pages in the notebook and exuberantly let out some of his "hmm" and "Awe" terminology.

"Come to think of it Katie . . ." He reached over and tapped her arm. "A good buddy of mine, who's actually my best friend from college, owns a publishing house here in Connecticut. This notebook is full of great stories. Your son is very talented because he goes deep into a character and displays great narratives in every scene."

Katie bobbled her head slightly. She only understood half of what Mr. Sordun just said as he continued speaking.

"I also know this talented ghost writer who lives in Hartford and I heard last week that he's looking for some action. Your son's diary could be that action. What do think?"

Katie swallowed hard feeling too emotional to speak. All she did was nod. A sudden increase of emotion sparked her thoughts to cease and assist with such jargon. Her son was her priority and by no means was she going to agree to anything without his permission. Katie swallowed again.

"Thank you sir for the wonderful words and thoughts. I can't give you an answer until I get Aiden's decision." She reached over and closed the notebook before she slid it closer. "I promise to give you an answer next week."

"Sounds great. I hope you have a great picnic and I'll see you both next week." Mr. Sordun cheered with his margarita, as he stood tall and headed to the next table.

"Thanks Mr. Magnum P.I.!" Michael loudly said.

Mr. Sordun spun around, still stepping backward, and placed a large cigar within his smile before he resumed his entourage visits.

Katie felt herself shake in disgust and joy. She truly didn't know how to take what just happened with Mr. Sordun being the first to read Aiden's diary and recommending it get published. The diary was in her hands but she still didn't find it appropriate to open this notebook without her son's permission. Abrupt, astute, and every adjective she could think circled in Katie's thoughts. Why? How? What for? She suddenly lost her insight pulling her deeper into how she was going to present this to her son.

Michael leaned inward and ran his hands along her arms. "It's OK Katie. It's OK. Let yourself and Aiden have a fun day at the picnic. When you get home, or even tomorrow, talk to him about what just happened and let him decide where you both are headed."

Her lips grew in size as she smiled. "Thanks for understanding this Michael."

"You would do the same for me Katie. How about we get another tasty beverage."

"Sounds like a winner and thanks again."

Michael blinked. "You're already a winner and will find that out later . . ."

CHAPTER TWENTY-NINE

The drive home felt long and surreal, as both Katie and Aiden didn't say much to each other. It was a fun filled day as Katie conversed with all her co-workers and Aiden spent wondrous time with Meghan. There were many good things too share with each other but neither could figure out the best way of explaining it.

Katie never felt so close to Michael as she did that day. Meeting his daughter was energizing, Meghan is a wonderful and lovely person. Her father is one heck of a man to raise such a stunning daughter.

And then there was the diary, the one she needed to talk with Aiden about. How can she explain that someone has already read his diary and that person now wants to get Aiden's personal punishment and relief tool published and viewed by all? This was oxy-moronic in so many ways and required some aspirin when she got home. Just the thought of all these situations made her giggle repetitiously with fear and happiness. Which one will it be? No matter what Aiden will be told. Katie's thoughts went round and round in circles.

Everything has changed, hasn't it? Aiden pondered staring straight ahead in silence. Many of his past daydreams held special places for Meghan. He couldn't discern why it was Meghan specifically and no other girls he came into contact with. He melted his stature upon seeing her every moment in the past. Today was special and soothing to best describe what happened. First he was shocked that Meghan's father was dating his mother. Even more shocking was the fact that he couldn't put all that together before today. He knew better than that and kicked himself just thinking about it.

All that didn't matter. Today was by far the best day Aiden has had in many years. Just being in shock must have unbolted his personal vault. Meghan did the greatest of things and talked openly to him. She was the most caring person to take control and calm him down for a fun-filled day of games and getting to know who she really was. He had always wanted it to be like that, just like that. He remembered his past daydreams that involved Meghan a hundred times before it actually happened and now its reality. But that reality felt eerie too him knowing friendship, possibly sisterhood, was the future. That sure offset his dreaming.

CHAPTER THIRTY

Aiden and Katie unpacked the car in utter silence as both carried their bags and food into the house with envy about what was going to be said. It showed in each other's facial expressions, one's that displayed stares added with half smiles.

They packed away the bags and placed the goodies into the refrigerator for their later treats. Mom started the coffee maker and hung in the kitchen for a few minutes. A French roasted coffee sent delightful smells into Aiden's nostrils and calmed his feelings a bit.

He then took a seat at the dining table and stared at the wall. He couldn't think of anything to say. But that was not entirely true. There were several hundred things to say and half of them he viewed as unsuitable and half were downright questionable to his mother's happiness. He openly enjoyed their friendship and knew it best to be honest with his mother. That's exactly what she enlightened him with numerous times. It's just this situation with Meghan enforced verbal hesitation and sent shivers through his body.

He then sighed as his mother took her seat across the table. *Here we go.* Aiden swished around in his chair contemplating his first discussion, one that he knew meant the world for many reasons. He held his tongue seeing his mother's eyes grow larger. He thought with enviable speed then abruptly came to a crashing halt. It was time to explain.

"Thanks for bringing me to the picnic today Mom, I had a fun time." His voice was not as steady as he wanted it to be and let out a deep breath.

Mom slightly nodded her head with a smile. She then sipped her coffee.

"It was a great day. We had wonderful conversation with others and the food was ever so yummy."

Aiden raised his eyes as he deemed his belly being full. "The food was great." He rubbed his tummy. "I don't think I could eat dinner tonight."

"We do have leftovers so eat some if you get hungry. No worries though I will make us some cheesy omelet's tomorrow morning."

Aiden's mouth drooped open. "Omelets? I cannot remember the last time you made those."

Mom displayed a forgiving expression. "I'm sorry pumpkin. I know it's been a while since our last flavorsome breakfast. I promise to fill our bellies tomorrow."

He didn't know why, he couldn't figure how it happened, but Aiden made his mother feel guilty. For no reason did he mean for that to happen. Something so simple and minor was breakfast guilt. When it came to their lives this was as little as a single strand of grass. That's how he perceived it. Besides, he had something to get off his chest.

Aiden slowly stood up and moved closer to his mother. He bent down and kissed her cheek as he handed her the diary. It was time for his mother to see all the dreams he's been experiencing and time for him to unload his internal guilt related to his personal isolation and horrid school grades. He then pulled a chair out next to her and crossed his legs.

"Please read my diary Mom. I just feel it's time for you to see what I've been dreaming about these past few months." He spoke in an honest fashion, one that widened his mother's eyes.

Handing off his recent dreaming experiences overwhelmed Katie for a few seconds. She sat motionless leading to the happiest exuberance she ever felt or experienced. A floating motion lifted her emotions into liveliness. She reached over and planted a big kiss on her son's lips. He sat back and stared at the diary.

Katie's fingers were trembling as she opened the diary to its first page. Knowing this diary meant everything to her son made her shiver for a moment. Her eyes began to swell up. Aiden then leaned forward.

"I have to tell you something before you read the diary." Aiden's posture stiffened. Yearning filled his stare. "There are many dreams about Meghan in the diary." He then hesitated for second. "I mean . . ." His face spurned a flare. "I honestly don't know how I thought of Meghan."

She watched his eyes drift away. That's something she never got used to seeing. No matter who it was, seeing someone in front of you disappear and recede into themselves was powerful and could mean a ton of things. Katie then quickly pondered what her son was saying. He obviously felt out of the ordinary in regards to Meghan. There was a possibility he thought more about Meghan than she ever knew about. Anything was possible with another person's interest. Katie just wondered if her current relationship with Meghan's father meant something more that she realized it was.

For the briefest of moments the muscles in Katie's neck tightened. "Are you OK with me dating Meghan's father?" she asked, trying to sound as though she was open minded. She regrettably hoped his answer was positive.

Aiden nodded. "Yes, It's great to see your happiness with Michael and I don't think anything bad about you two being together. It's just that I've thought a lot about Meghan and can't figure out why my feelings for her have been so strong." He then hesitated for second. His facial expression mirrored a light bulb being flicked on. "Maybe my daydreams are predictions about my future. It means more than I can understand."

Katie sighed in joy. Her son was a saint who astounded her every minute of every day. She often wondered how such a profound and wonderful child birthed from her womb. Aiden was a gift.

"I love you Aiden and especially love who you are. Your daydreams are so powerful. I could see it in your face when you fell into them. Every dream you had meant more than any person could comprehend or analyze. I just hope your dreams help you in many ways."

"I hope so too." Aiden said as he looked down to the diary.

It was maybe a few seconds' later—pins and needles tingled her innards—when Katie realized she was not the first one, other than Aiden, to read his diary. She promised herself that she would tell him about this. She sure was. A deep breath was taken.

"I won't be the first person who read a little of your diary." Katie felt at peace and continued. "Earlier today when you and Meghan were playing in the field I made sure to keep your diary close but my boss, Mr. Sordun, read through some pages when Michael and I were distracted. I quivered in angst for not telling him how private your diary was."

Aiden clinched his eyebrows then smiled. "It's OK. I'm not hiding anything."

"Mr. Sordun also mentioned something about getting your diary published into primetime. I guess it would be similar to those Danielle Steel novels I read. He knows many people in that industry and mentioned that he's got friends that can handle this." Katie looked deep into his eyes. "Are you OK with this?"

Aiden sat back and vibrantly spun his thoughts for a few seconds before he reminisced with a chuckle.

"That's wicked cool! I can only imagine being J.R.R. Tolkien." He abruptly stood and spun on one foot. "I'll be Frodo Baggins and carry the ring of authorship around the Shire." Aiden then began portraying a Hobbit as he wide footed around the dining room and loosely curled his fingers to fashion a pipe.

Katie's eyes grew wider. She remembered gifting Aiden with the Lord of the Rings trilogy several years ago and never contemplated him reading and remembering so much from the novels. It didn't matter her son was animated and spread joy around the room.

This day's happiness, if it was only her son's excited emotions, easily exceeded every cautious thought Katie had.

CHAPTER THIRTY-ONE

The following workweek was blurry. It took Katie a few days to realize what just happened. She passed Mr. Sordun the diary on Monday and was handed back the following day with a wink. The computer screen was fuzzy as she contemplated the sequence of events that transpired with the ghostwriter accepting the project with full steam. He projected a completion in a few days time.

Never the less, the diary was finished and it was only Friday. What a week. Mr. Sordun then mentioned this morning that the publisher in Connecticut accepted the novel and will begin in record speed to distribute and market to the world. This corporate pace astonished Katie and made her relish next to nothing with the amount of information being passed to her.

She passed the knowledge to Aiden every night and he gripped every word with anticipation. His eyes were enthralled. That's something Katie never got used to but sure did suck in all the joy both of them were experiencing. Watching your son's posture straighten and his emotions grow ten times higher meant nothing but happiness. Her son was exuberant and that meant everything to a mother.

Katie shook her head, as she stood tall and headed to the break room for another coffee. All these rapid events spun her emotions and thoughts into a further blur.

Her focus dwindled her work but she stayed abrupt to accomplish as much as she could. Caffeine was needed.

As she grabbed the coffee pot and poured a further amount than usual Katie heard someone step into the room.

"Greetings to my best friend." Michael mentioned in a positive stance.

"Hello my love. Hope your day is going well?" Katie glanced back with a wink.

"Oh, it's another day." He said in a soured tone but fantastic smile. "Have you heard anything from your family about the vacation?"

Michael's sincere curiosity quickly disarmed Katie— she had a vast amount of good news. Shirley and Pete informed her last night that the trailer was free and clear for vacation use next week. The trailer was in a reasonable location along the Maine coast, one that was financially acceptable and had many fun events for the children. Katie felt comfort knowing the good news was about to be passed.

"Yes." Katie winked again with an excited facial stare. "Are you ready to go?"

"I'm already packed and ready to relax." He raised a hand to his hip. "The car is serviced and is ready to roll whenever you're ready." A sudden abrupt eyebrow lift portrayed hesitation. "Meghan is excited but no where near being packed. I throw her hints everyday to make sure she remembers. She just happens to be a last minute packer."

"Michael, your daughter is a woman and most don't consider their travel needs while packing, they make their clothing items a priority. I would know that very well since I could be held guilty for last minute packing. There were many trips where I purchased items at the vacation site. It's just how us women operate." Katie took a sip of her coffee and jetted a grin. "However, I'm already packed and ready to go as well." She then giggled.

"How about Aiden, is he excited and ready?"

"You better believe he is. He's been asking me these past few nights if I needed any help packing. He's quite the helper bee."

Michael nodded. "Yes you are my adored dating princess."

"Well aren't you cute."

Some steps were heard getting closer. Katie noticed Mr. Sordun enter the room with a large smile, one that showed interest but also tiredness. It was Friday and that meant a rested weekend was needed, especially for the head of this company. Katie pulled out the empty coffee pot.

"Good afternoon sir. You look tired and I can make some more coffee if you need some?"

Mr. Sordun's smile drooped to a straight face. "No thanks Katie. If I have more caffeine I think I'll shake beyond belief and get no sleep tonight. Besides, I'm taking the better half out for an elegant dinner tonight."

"Sounds like a great night is ahead." Michael bobbed his head softly.

"I hope it will be. Having a corporate dinner tonight at Yankee Peddler and just hope dinner is served fast because I'm already hungry to say the least."

His thoughts then seemed to drift away. Katie found his emotional shift surreal. Mr. Sordun's clear-headed thinking and honesty were all she knew. Even Michael showed some interest. Katie felt obligated to ask something, she's seen that off-the-wall thinking pattern being displayed on Mr. Sordun many times.

"Is there something we can do for you?"

"No, no, I'm fine Katie." Mr. Sordun lamented at first then smiled. "I just have a thousand things going on right now and wish I was prioritizing these events better than I can." He slowly shook his head. "Ah, that's enough of me venting. I'm jealous of both of you. You're vacation starts next week, right?"

Katie smirked. "It sure does."

"Both of you deserve that vacation and you two are some of my favorites." A stern facial expression then formed. "Now, don't let that inflate your noggins." He winked as he pointed to both of them.

Michael threw-up his arms. "We surrender Mr. Sordun, we surrender! And promise to return with more energy."

Katie noticed Mr. Sordun's latent facial expression even though he did grin a little. An overwhelming need to assist her boss flew through her thoughts. He was a man she respected and actually liked. He was a true professional and one that surprised many who worked in former companies laden with jerks and off-the-wall bosses. He was unique to say the least and that made Katie feel comfortable in this building. Her internal thoughts were never revealed though, she just couldn't remember informing any co-workers about her opinion. Well, there was Michael, but he was her best friend.

"Is everything OK?" Katie placed her hand on Michael's shoulder but stared ahead. "We are pretty good listeners and can help you anyway we can."

Mr. Sordun's eyes cast down as he pinched his lips. "I don't want to bore the both of you by expressing this matter but getting it off my chest will help." He then looked up with a grin. "Plus, I can say this with no worries because both of you aren't soap opera types. Bottom line is that my son quit college and is moving out to Los Angeles to hunt down an acting role and play music. My wife told me he took my brother's guitar and that Flamenco styled guitar has been in the family for generations. It has such a beautiful cypress body and spruce top and has been polished beyond belief . . ."

Katie and Michael quickly glanced at each other with open eyes. She then took a step forward.

"Sorry to hear that. Is there anything we can do to help?"

Mr. Sordun blinked with an embellished stare. He then daunted a look of guilt. "Oh, I'm OK. To be honest, I don't blame my son for taking charge of his life's ambitions. He's young, dumb, and full of energy. I was the father that ordered his childhood activities and school courses. Per my direction he conducted sporting events and was on teams while in school. During his free time he played instruments and I brushed that to the side." Mr. Sordun then shook his head. "I'm guilty of forcing my son to not be who he is. He rebelled in his growing years and I honestly don't blame him. I screwed-up and actually regret myself for that. I can only imagine what my son will think about me for the rest of his life."

Katie stood in silence for a few seconds. She glanced over to Michael and he portrayed a look of trepidation. This was Mr. Sordun, a professional man who mainly spurted out quick jokes and directions to his supervisors. His open candor was surprising to say the least.

She then questioned herself but didn't know why. She only knew what Mr. Sordun mentioned about his children and just the thought of ordering children in their growing years didn't make sense to her. Katie then remembered that her father was similar. But she was raised in the 60's and that meant rebellion for personal freedom and was supported by her sisters and friends.

"Please know that Michael and I understand what your saying." Michael nodded slowly as Katie earnestly spoke. "To be honest with you Mr. Sordun, your son is lucky to have a mother and father because he had two parents to talk to, ask questions, and learn from."

Katie saw skepticism mixed with hope in Mr. Sordun's eyes.

"I guess your right. I was the bad cop and my wife the good cop. My son sure did have us no matter what. I guess I will always wonder if I parented my son right," he told her as his persona and facial expression changed.

Michael then stepped forward. "We are here for you if you need us sir."

"Ah, it's OK and I will be fine." He then winked. "Now, both of you have fun on your vacation." Mr. Sordun then began heading toward the door. "Oh, Katie, I almost forgot to tell you. I just received a call from my publishing friend and he said your novel is being edited this weekend and ready for distribution by the end of next week."

Katie instantly felt an emotional bombardment flow through her body as Michael wrapped his arm around her shoulders and pulled her closer. He then kissed her cheek as Mr. Sordun waved his hand and continued out the door.

CHAPTER THIRTY-TWO

A week at the beach filled with excitement and activities drew everyone closer to each other. Of course, what Mom mentioned *"We need a vacation from our vacation"* was the truth. There was a different sight seeing location everyday of the week. Up and down route 1 in Maine and New Hampshire engulfed the trip and everyone saw locations they always contemplated visiting.

Aiden held a questionable thought within the back of his brain, one that intrigued him internally to the point of nervousness and wonderment. He hasn't daydreamed in several weeks. He couldn't understand or explain why he lost that connection, but he did know that a lot of energy and activities these past weeks tunneled his thoughts. Those thoughts were compelling to the point of exhaustion.

Michael was an energetic man, one who planned all their activities for week's prior—or so it seems. Aiden wondered halfway through the vacation how all these sights and attractions were thought about or known. He hesitated in asking Michael because he was a true historian, one who blatantly exuded all the unknown specifics to every location they visited or spent time in.

While visiting Old Orchard Beach, just to the east of Saco, Maine, Michael expressed how Charles Lindbergh stopped on this beach in 1927 on his trans-Atlantic flight from New York to Paris. He also took them to Perkins Cove in Ogunquit and brought them to all the wondrous sites, shops, and alcoves where he mentioned actresses like Sally Struthers and Bette Davis used to visit continuously. This was their summer sanctuary. Michael also interested Aiden when he mentioned that Stephen King's The Stand's contrived location was set in Ogunquit as well.

Aiden was amazed because he loved history and never would of thought of researching that information unless he was directed to. He definitely learned quite a bit form Michael's energetic and profound story telling, one's that kept everyone enticed and wanting more. That's how Aiden took it because he noticed Meghan and Mom kept walking or headed to dip their toes in the frigid water on the Maine coastline. It was summer and the Maine's ocean was still chilled to the point of redness and numbness if in too deep or for too long. Several minutes seemed too many.

Every morning, before sunrise, coffee was brewing and the parents were off for their morning walks. Upon their return Meghan would roll out of her bed and get herself ready as Aiden followed suit and accompanied her for their morning strolls along Long Sands beach. He didn't know why he just internally felt it best to delay his excitement and let Meghan lead the way. The last thing he wanted her to think was that he was arduous or annoying so he followed her stride.

Both of them grabbed their plastic handled buckets and carefully walked the embankment down to the darkish colored clay beach. The entire week's morning's sky was vividly blue and reflected in the water that broke gently against the shoreline. Timing was perfect because every morning was low tide and the long expanse of muddy hard beach was tranquil and filled with shells and sea dollars.

When they returned to the campgrounds Meghan and Aiden would show each other their seashell treasure chest and count their sea dollars for the daily win. *She sure is the lucky one.* Aiden thought constantly as she beat him every morning.

The best was the fact that Meghan was an open flower and shared all her emotions and thoughts. Aiden felt closely connected to her faster than any other friend he ever had. She asked a lot about him and Aiden always spoke the truth. What enticed him greater was that Meghan listened and didn't hold anything against him. She provided her viewpoint every time he asked for it and regardless she was a cordial and open-minded person and that was a personality he always strove for.

To top the whole week and make it the most memorable Michael enticed several of the campground neighbors into throwing a clambake on the beach. He got the camp and local authorities permission and gathered all the items that were needed. He then invited the local Veteran's of Foreign Wars Post to the event and many showed and contributed food and beverages.

It was their final night and that clambake was unbelievable to Aiden. The amount of food and joy was conducted and led by Michael. A glowing ambience brought smiles upon Aiden's face as the steamer clams, fresh mussels, lobsters, and corn in the husk was served in copious amounts to all who attended.

Not only was this a vacation this was a new moment Aiden had dreamt of his whole life. Michael and Meghan now felt like a father and sister to him. They were that close too him now in astonishment.

CHAPTER THIRTY-THREE

As Katie and Aiden arrived home, they unpacked, opened the windows, started the laundry and passed to each other their enjoyable vacation with smiles and winks. The phone rang and Michael informed Katie that they made it home free-and-clear of any problems and looked forward to seeing her next week at work.

Katie then noticed the answering machine was blinking. She pressed the button and heard a few voicemails from her sisters who all sounded joyous and asked for callbacks. Then there were voicemails from a few co-workers who passed congratulations. A few of her close friends, ones she hasn't talked to in quite some time, also wished her best wishes.

What is going on with all this? Katie thought as she walked back into the dinning room. She unpacked the laundry bag and separated the light and dark clothing as she opened the washer machine door. She then noticed Aiden walking around her and it instantly felt like a brute force slapped her sub consciousness to reality.

"Oh my god! Oh my lord!" Katie's voice progressed louder with each word.

Aiden turned around in the hallway and bent his head with an inquisitive stare. "What's wrong Mom? Is something happening?"

All of a sudden the phone started to ring, as Katie stood tall. She thought both ways first to either answer her son or the phone. She was bamboozled and didn't know which path took precedence. She leaned to her left, then to her right, before she stood still and took a deep breath before she looked at Aiden.

"Hold on honey. I'll tell you once I get off the phone."

Katie walked into the living room, took a seat on the couch, and pleasingly picked-up the phone. "Hello". She then heard a graceful French accented voice, one that she instantly identified. "Uncle Romeo, it's great to hear from you." Romeo owned the Odyssey Bookstore in South Hadley, MA and Katie normally saw him once a year at family picnics and gatherings. He mentioned that he just received his weekly book distribution and noticed a novel named The Daydreamer's Diary and the author's name was Aiden Ellis. "That is my son Uncle Romeo." Seconds of silence then passed and anticipation grew tremendously within Katie. This was the most silence she ever could imagine from her uncle.

Aiden then walked into the living room and took a seat next to Katie with his lips slightly parted and his head tilted to the side. These made Katie feel better knowing she wasn't the only one experiencing anticipation.

"Uh huh." Katie answered as Uncle Romeo's verbal tone flamboyantly increased. He mentioned the curiosity at the same time he mentioned his excitement. It was wondrous to hear her uncle's animated expressions—one's that always enticed her sisters and family.

Uncle Romeo asked if the following weekend was vacant on her schedule for a book signing at his store. He mentioned how proud he would be to have a direct family member be presented to all who showed.

Katie took in all the conversation with elevated cheeks. She could tell her smile was larger than life due to her chin and other facial muscles beginning to cramp. All this enthusiasm and stimulation was centered on her son. Aiden sat next to her and his lower lip began to tremble in anticipation. Katie winked as Uncle Romeo finished his kind words.

"Definitely and we thank you Uncle Romeo. My son, the author, and I look forward to seeing you next weekend. I promise to let everyone know about the special event. Bye."

Aiden's head swiveled and his face grew redder as Katie hung-up the phone. She sat for a minor second, one that felt like forever, putting all this great information together for its presentation to her son. All this thought and all this glory sped her heart rate. This was by far the most astonishing and telltale moment in her parenting life. She took a long breath.

"I want to congratulate you on becoming the first Author in our family. Your new book is called The Daydreamer's Diary and it's been published and distributed out to bookstores. That was Uncle Romeo and he asked if you would be available next weekend for a book signing in his store." Katie winked with a smile. "What do you think?"

Aiden slid lower into the couch and stretched out his legs under the coffee table. He then stared at the ceiling with a tattered facial look of confusion. That look was brief. He then shot forward in amazement and banged his knees under the table. A few empty glasses and objects rolled and flew off the table's front side.

"Wow", then an "Ouch" as he rubbed his kneecaps for a second or two, followed by a "Wicked Cool" sprouted from the most excited facial expression ever seen from her son. Katie jumped up without even thinking about it and danced a few small circles with Aiden before he skipped down the hallway with elegant grace and a stumble as he tripped a few times over his feet.

CHAPTER THIRTY-FOUR

The Odyssey Bookstore was filled with patrons and family members who gazed around at "The Daydreamer's Diary" advertisements that were enlarged and placed in-and-around the store area. The interior was delightfully decorated with exquisite ornaments and famous book covered posters that laden the walls. A large area that encompassed the entire bottom floor to the bookstore was filled with rows of chairs and a one-leveled stage that occupied an elegantly laced mahogany wooded podium.

The official book signing was about to begin and the room was filled with family and friends in several of the front rows. Many decided to arrive early to get closer to stage seats for such an event adding to family significance.

Katie knew she had a seat close to the stage but devoted herself to standing in the back of the room to meet all who entered. There were many faces and names she never recognized and that enticed her to meet them all.

Her cousin was a professional photographer and graciously agreed to take pictures for this memorable day. Larry was all over the room snapping away the ambience and faces that encompassed the entire bookstore.

In the center of the room were many co-workers and former classmates Katie respected, they sure lived up to their promises of attendance. Just the fact of seeing people she hasn't encountered in years added to her excitement.

The room was filled quickly and Katie suddenly heard a recognizable voice walking down the stairs. It was Mr. Sordun with his wife and two individuals she didn't recognize. Katie moved to the foot of the stairway.

"Good afternoon Mr. and Mrs. Sordun." Katie said with a slight nod.

"There she is!" Mr. Sordun mentioned with a pleasant voice. He then reached the floor and pointed to his left with a large grin. "Katie, I'd like to introduce you to the two most significant gentlemen who helped accomplish this goal." He placed his hand on the first man's shoulder. "This is a great friend of mine, Joe Marois, who owns the publishing company that worked this novel."

Mr. Marois reached out and Katie shook his sturdy gripped hand. Mr. Sordun then pointed towards the next gentleman who winked an impressive stare.

"And this is Wayne Hudson, the one and only ghost writer who transcribed your son's novel from pen to paper." Mr. Mosley stylishly held his hand in a horizontal position. Katie stood there for a second before she placed her hand underneath and tilted into a handshake. Mr. Sordun blasted out a strong smirk. "He's quite the artsy fartsy type Katie and one heck of a great writer."

Katie blinked in amazement. "Thank you all for this and what you've done for my son. I truly can't thank you enough, but please feel free to take a seat in the front of the room." Katie pointed down the row of chairs and watched them delightfully head in that direction.

There was so much to be said and so many thoughts to be shared with those gentlemen and Katie knew it was near the starting time for this event. She was bewildered by how fast all these events happened.

All of sudden a side door opened and Katie perched a large smile seeing her cousin Joan lead Aiden closer both hand-to-hand. Joan was practicing with Aiden for the book signing presentation. Joan was Romeo's daughter and that enforced Katie's secure feelings knowing that her son was guided well for this event.

As they passed closer Katie locked her eyes with Aiden as he bestowed a quick grin. She could only imagine the tenseness and anxiety her son was experiencing. She felt the same and was with him. He was about to discern his novel contents to his family, friends, and local populace.

Katie was in la la land. This event was by far the most exciting event in her life and one to be forever remembered.

CHAPTER THIRTY-FIVE

As Joan directed him to the stage Aiden stared straight ahead feeling numb. This was it, his book signing, one he didn't dream or know about till days prior. Anxiety, mystery, ignorance, and reality all combined into one.

Joan introduced herself and welcomed the audience as Aiden stared straight ahead in the crowded room and took his seat next to the podium. He felt his blood pressure boost as Joan raised the book, and raised it high, explaining the synopsis to the story and how it disembarked to this very moment. She then told the audience about the book's contents and filtered down into descriptions and narratives. Aiden was impressed with Joan who verbally lured the audience into flamboyant attention. She then read out a daydream segment:

"A brisk chill in the nighttime air brought the chipmunk family out of their burrow to chirp in safety. Bright stars above aligned in unison and increased their apparent magnitude into a single beam. Under that beam were a mother and her litter. Their hunger was obvious seeing their rib cages reflect in the light. As the chipmunks grew closer together, their family love sparked a flow of nuts and berries being highlighted for harvest. Their love power increased their survival many folds. It was a true blessing . . ."

This inspired Aiden to drift away into daydream questions. Why so many this past year? There has to be some kind of reason? He whirled around for a second or two and then realized he hasn't read the professionally written version to his diary. He half-heartedly listened to what Joan was vocalizing, but comprehended most of it. Her voice was so tranquil and comforting. It's just that he didn't know what some of the words meant but they sure did flow together well.

He shook his head to push away the distracting questions and thoughts. It was impossible to ignore the reason he was there. He then raised his eyes and noticed instant smiles and winks directed at him as he visually scanned the room. He then contemplated his looks. Maybe his nose twisted in sneer, or his tongue protruded out of his mouth like a dog infesting on a bone or cookie. He could only imagine what people would think if he perched a ragged facial expression in the middle of his book signing.

He then came to grips, his family was attending and that meant love and support, ones he experienced his whole life. He then remembered what Joan mentioned to him earlier and how he was going to recite a dream from his novel. Joan made sure to place a sticker in its location and informed him of its significant color being blue. How could he forget that, blue was his favorite color.

Aiden then visually searched the room and saw his mother standing in the back of the room. Her exuberant smile felt so close as if she was directly in front of him. He knew he was next to read to the audience another segment from his novel and squirmed that around and around in his mind in hoping he would conduct it without stuttering or hesitating. He then looked at his mother again and this feeling of strength and joy reinforced his successful feeling.

Joan then finished another segment as the audience clapped with smiles and elation. She then placed her hand on Aiden's shoulder and mentioned that he was going to recite the following dream before the book signing. The audience was then told that the table adjacent to their left, she pointed over, was the location where Aiden would signature all the novels.

She then stepped away and pushed a stepping stool behind the podium. Aiden nervously stood to his feet and stepped upon the stool as Joan pulled the microphone down lower and pointed to the blue sticker. He nodded his head in acceptance while Joan winked a loving expression before she headed to a reserved seat in the front row.

Aiden then cleared his throat and welcomed everyone. He thanked all for attending his book signing before he took a deep breath and began reading from his diary. As he started to read he somehow heard a voice within that told him he was reading too fast. His cognizance often corrected his actions, ones he just never thought deeply about but enjoyed. After several paragraphs Aiden then realized his voice was not as steady as he wanted it to be, he was moving along and close to the finish.

CHAPTER THIRTY-SIX

Katie was so proud to hear Aiden present his words pleasantly. He just seemed comfortable and drew the audience into desiring more daydreams. The look upon their faces was astonishing. It was as if her son was a rock star. Ah! He was to her. Katie's hands shivered in delight as her legs became weak. She told herself to take comfort and sit, she just couldn't move.

As soon as Aiden finished his segment the crowd jumped to their feet and clapped loudly before whistling and expressing their love and support. Katie felt her innards shiver with joy as Joan escorted him to the table.

But then, suddenly, Aiden looked her way in excitement and darted from the stage heading her direction. At the same time Katie smelt the eloquent Old Spice fragrance and jetted her head over to see Michael with Meghan. She reached over and planted a fervent hug on him before tears began to flow down her face. Michael tapped her back lightly.

"Hello and sorry we're late."

"It's OK. I understand you were attending Meghan's piano class." Katie said while swabbing her cheeks along her sleeves.

"This event is amazing. There are so many people and the atmosphere here is joyous . . . Oomph!"

Aiden jumped on to Michael's side and grabbed him tightly. Michael spun around and squatted lower followed by a large hug. They both stood tall before Meghan hugged Aiden deeply then planted a kiss to his cheek. A telltale flush appeared on his neckline and worked its way to his face.

Katie stood back and took all this in. It made her feel surreal with a level of comfort she never experienced before. Aiden was so attached to Michael and Meghan and that clearly was evident how family-like this appeared.

This drew Katie into blissful seconds before a sudden rush of Patchouli scent blew closer and closer. An overwhelming hesitation spurned her emotions with anxiety and disgust. She swallowed hard and turned her head slowly.

The look upon Stewart's face was one of shock. His mouth dropped wide open with eyebrows literally raised to his hairline. Katie hesitated for a second in disbelief that Stewart actually showed. She wasn't expecting this whatsoever. No communication between the two of them happened since he moved to Virginia. This quickly made her wonder how he knew and what could possibly motivate such a visit. Katie hoped it was Aiden but experience wise she knew there was probably another person he was visiting as well. *What timing!* Katie quivered.

She took a few steps forward but again she hesitated. It was impossible to ignore the reason he was there. Stewart kept his stare on Aiden and blinked a few looks into Katie's eyes.

"Hello Katie."

"What are you doing here Stewart?" Katie then realized what she'd said and how he might have perceived it. The eerie thoughts of why he was here for Aiden's significant event overwhelmed her. The last thing she wanted was her son's day being spun around in emotional circles. Stewart's presence gnawed at her.

Stewart then smirked. "What do you think Katie? I'm here to see my son and congratulate him for such an accomplishment."

Katie made sure to provide a glum stare to make him feel guilty as Stewart just looked around her to lure Aiden's attention. Katie then noticed her son standing by her side. Stewart held his arms out.

"Hello my son, congratulations!"

Aiden took a few slower steps closer as Stewart tugged him in for a hug. He stood loose with arms dangling as Stewart lifted him high.

"It's so great to see you." Stewart released him gently. He then leaned back and kept his hands upon Aiden's shoulders. "I heard about this event yesterday and drove nine hours to be here and support you."

Katie could see her son's loose stature and straight legs displayed his bewilderment. She instinctually knew it best to pull Stewart to the side so Aiden could begin his book signing. The majority of the audience looked back while the others got in line for the signing. *This event needed to move forward*. Katie thought as she stepped forward and pulled Aiden closer to her. She then looked back and winked at Michael.

"Please escort Aiden to the table. My cousin Joan will be there to help start the signings."

Michael nodded as he stepped closer. He put his hand on Aiden's head and swished his hair a few times. "Let's go Tiger. It's time for you to become an accomplished author and impress the crowd."

Katie then looked at Stewart in disgust. By no means was she expecting this moment.

"Why are you taking him away from me?" His voice was taut with questionable irritation. It was anger because Katie exclusively remembered that voice during every argument leading to their divorce.

"I apologize, timing is not right. Aiden is expected to sign his books for the audience. You will have more than enough time after this event is finished."

She then contemplated his presence and calmed a bit. Just being here for his son's magnificent event meant something pleasant. Katie then sensed Stewart's surly attitude. She identified that look.

Frustration was a tough feeling to conceal. One that Katie reminded herself, all the time, not to let anyone she was against witness. She viewed it as a sign of drawback and weakness and one that would hamper her stance. She would have to rebuild or start from scratch. Stewart then crossed his arms.

"I'm going to have to hit the road tonight because I have work tomorrow morning." Stewart's head was still as he blinked repeatedly. "My long drive here was for my son and by god I deserve more time with him."

Katie felt confused. That's not who Stewart was and what he said is not true. She couldn't remember him taking a trip for one event or person. She opened her mouth as she squinted at him. Stewart tossed a glance at her and rolled his eyes before returning his attention to Aiden and the audience.

She then questioned herself for sending Aiden away so fast. Maybe he could have spent a few more minutes with Stewart. Maybe I could have informed the audience that Aiden's father was visiting. Katie then told herself to stop thinking this stuff when she realized Stewart had gotten over her wall somehow. She took a deep breath and kept her voice low.

"Aiden is your son, but you had so many hours, days, and years to spend time with him."

Stewart then portrayed a questionable look. "Look Katie, I'm his father and I have every right to spend time with my son."

"Sure, whenever you want to spend time with our son." Katie felt her forehead wrinkle. "Is his full-time mother here to beckon any request for you?"

Stewart raised an eyebrow and kept silent as he turned to view the audience.

Her blood pressure peaked. She could feel her neck throb. But then she took a deep breath and contemplated why she was feeling this way. This event, this day, was for Aiden and only Aiden. By no means was she supposed to be this upset when her focus should be her son. Reality hit her innards like a baseball bat. Katie knew this was her son's decision, not hers, to spend time with his father. She was his mother not his dominating matriarch.

Katie told herself to relax and reinforced a calming voice.

"Thanks for being here Stewart. I'm sure your son will appreciate your presence." Katie noticed Stewart bobbing his head. "After the book signing I will let you spend as much time as Aiden wants to spend with you. It's his call."

Stewart shot a quick glance her way. "You're a good woman Katie."

Chapter Thirty-Seven

The book signing was enjoyable as Aiden received many loving and friendly comments from the audience. As the line got smaller he could feel his pen holding fingers get weak. He lost count of his signings after thirty or so. But that didn't matter this event was exciting and he loved being thought of by all who attended.

When the last person thanked him and expressed how proud they were Aiden stared off into grateful bliss. He told himself that he would never forget this day because all these wondrous moments were special. Family, friends, school kids, fire fighters, police officers, and most importantly Meghan and Michael were there. This event was far too large for him to recognize all who attended but it sure was blissful to say the least.

He then noticed Joan cleaning up the table and stacking the unsold books into a mobile bookrack. Her compassion and support truly showed how important and amorous his family was. Aiden knew that his family builds internal strength and motivation to go forth and achieve personal goals. He grabbed Joan's wrist.

"Thanks Auntie Joan for today and who you are."

Joan's facial glare increased with a large smile. "You would do the same for me Aiden."

Aiden stood to his feet and helped Joan pack the rest of the books and utensils into her box. He then assisted her in lowering the box to the floor followed by folding the table cloth and moving the table to the back of the stage. He wanted to help a person who helped him.

He then noticed his mother step on to the stage. Her face was filled with anxiety as she leaned down and kissed his cheek. Aiden smiled and tucked a deep hug around her. Her warmth and love filled his innards with gratification.

"Your father is sitting in the back of the room and would like to talk with you." She then waved her hand. "By no means does that mean you have to talk him. It's up to you and only you."

Aiden felt a shiver and didn't know why. He remembered nothing more than wishing more time being spent with his father. That felt like the past and he didn't know why. This raw feeling of contempt was new and confused Aiden. He knew his father was his father but he didn't know who he truly was.

"I'll talk with him mom." Aiden bobbed his head.

"OK kiddo. I'll be across the room with family if you need me."

Aiden then noticed his father stepping closer. What his mother just said "I'll be across the room with family . . ." kept repeating over and over again adding to his confusion. He always thought his father was his family. It then dawned on him. A sudden reality of who family truly are flickered through his thoughts. The dictionary and thesaurus mom provided him were great and he remembered researching that word specifically. There are so many differing definitions that it confused Aiden into believing 'family' was a personal perspective. Every person viewed a family differently.

His father then took a seat next to him. "You did such a wonderful job for someone so young. I'm proud to be your father." He exuded a large smile.

"Thanks."

Aiden then listened as dad, at first hesitantly, then in a rush of words, confessed to him about how proud he was of his son for contriving such wonderful words making it to the publishing industry. He kept mentioning how special his son was artistic wise and that he must have received those genes from his father. He went on and on bringing Aiden into uncomfortable feelings of not believing what he was being told.

Why should I believe in what he's saying? Aiden thought as he took this deep within his heart. He learned from his mother that trust and respect were earned. *What has dad done to deserve any of those?* Aiden now knew what was right and wrong when it came to understanding his parents and their extreme differences, especially who they are as individual people and personalities.

Aiden saw skepticism mixed with hope in his father's eyes. His facial expression was truly evident. Excitement was spread amongst everyone he could think of in his life, just not his father. All those thoughts, anticipations, and confusion about his father culminated into reality.

Dad then asked a question Aiden remembered his mother asking him: "Tell me about your daydreaming?" The tone in which dad asked the question felt like pressured curiosity. Aiden took it as such. He remembered his mother asking that same question followed by: "It's OK if you don't. No pressure." This sparked Aiden into remembrance of his daydreams and that his mother was supportive and loving during all while his father was distant and silent. Aiden felt it best not to answer he just sat in silence.

Dad looked at his watch. "I'm sorry son I have to hit the road and head back home. It's about a nine-hour drive and who knows what traffic will be. I have to work tomorrow morning to pay the bills."

Aiden perceived nothing but excuses. "OK, Have a safe trip."

As his father headed out the door Aiden relished the momentary light-heartedness he saw in his father's eyes. It was an instant reminder of how he now viewed his father as distant.

CHAPTER THIRTY-EIGHT

The following weeks were incredible to Aiden. As fall classes began he experienced a plethora of good comments and conversations with classmates he never spoke with. He knew that was minor fame due to his book sales doing well.

Aiden focused more attention with his current friends and school subjects. He also couldn't remember the last daydream he experienced and his attention during classroom instruction increased more than he thought. He truly felt that his next report card would make his mother smile. He knew that having someone watch over a subject or goal achievement kept him on course. And mom was by far the most trusted and best friend he ever could imagine.

Aiden tried out for football and made secondary team. He knew he wasn't in top shape or had the experience the first team had but the motivation to try something new enticed his play.

Meghan was truly a new best friend and they daily exchanged conversations and experiences with each other. Aiden met her other best friend and sat beside them on every bus ride to and from school.

What Aiden found to be the most interesting was when Meghan asked him about a boy in her class she was interested in dating. That was his first experience of a girl asking advice from him. Aiden knew that boy played on his football team and experienced the boy's attitude and asked him several questions before providing Meghan the thumbs-up.

Michael and mom were still dating and their relationship was truly a friendship followed by days of closeness. That was something Aiden didn't want to think too much about but Michael was the best guy he ever met and was inspired for more jokes and conversation from such an experienced man he was.